# Want Me, Cowboy

# *Want Me, Cowboy*

**A Copper Mountain Rodeo Romance**

Sinclair Jayne

TULE

PUBLISHING

Want Me, Cowboy

Tule Publishing First Printing, October 2016

The Tule Publishing Group, LLC



ISBN: 978-1-945879-39-5

# Prologue

LUKE WILDER TILTED his Stetson lower on his face and pushed open the double doors on Grey's Saloon and eyeballed the historic bar. If it had been any other bar in any other Montana town, he would have liked what he saw—a long battered bar that told a story and a worn, scuffed floor that told a thousand more—but this was Marietta, the one town and the one rodeo he'd avoided the entire ten years of his professional career.

*Sanctimonious, judgmental bastards.*

He went inside, letting the doors swing shut behind him. Eleven o'clock was early for a beer, but what the hell? It was Thursday. He was in town a day ahead of schedule. His trailer was already set up at the fair grounds for the rodeo. He was hungry. And thirsty. And meeting up with his mother after deftly avoiding her for the past two years definitely required a beer on board.

He hooked one boot on the rail under the bar, leaned against the scratched wood, and scanned what was on tap. Under the patina of history, Grey's looked a lot more upscale than most bars he'd been in during his rodeo days. His mom had said Marietta had changed so much she'd barely recognized it. A lot more boutiques and niche restaurants. The Graff hotel that had once been in total ruin had been renovated and was now featured in travel and design magazines and boasted more than a few celebrity sightings. His mom had sounded a bit disappointed when she'd told him, although his mother's slumming days were so far in her past she didn't seem to remember them. He did.

Frowning over his unusual burst of introspection, he ordered a Big Sky Scape Goat Pale Ale, not exactly local out of Missoula, but he had at least visited that town and liked it, and he'd spent many years as a scape goat for the antics of his younger brother, who'd managed to charm their mother while Luke had been heaped with responsibility, cooking and cleaning and watching his brother while his mother worked, attended school, and bounced between men. This late morning meeting with his mom made him feel like those memories might not be as far in the past as he'd like. The bartender, who slid the beer in front of him, looked as pissed off as Luke felt. Guilt and a misplaced sense of family duty were bitchy twins to carry around on his shoulders, and he was damned tired of the burden.

He avoided his mother and his brother for a reason.

He took a deep drink. Ordered a burger and fries. Avoided eye contact with the few other men sitting at the bar. None of the circuit cowboys had rolled into town yet.

They'd probably start arriving early to midday tomorrow, and then this town would feel a hell of a lot more comfortable, once he took care of the business that had brought him here.

His way. Not his mother's.

He'd experienced some peace in the last two years since he'd seen her, and he'd like to keep it that way.

"Hey, baby, what are you doing in here?" A breathless voice with a husky catch demanded behind him. Two slim, pale, bare arms slid around his waist, one palm flattened against his abs while the other stole his beer. "You finally broke down and tried a microbrew. Big Sky? Hmmmm. Delish, but Summer Honey is my favorite."

Her hand slid down his abs a bit lower, and Luke definitely felt his body respond to the hint.

"Bit early though." Again the husky voice caressed his ear, and he wasn't sure if she were implying a bit early for beer or for something more physically recreational, either one he was game. "But live a little, I guess."

*Definitely.*

He turned to face the thief. Tall. Slim. Legs that stretched forever under her short denim skirt. Crazy, blonde curls spilling everywhere. Blondes weren't necessarily his type, but a quick hookup would improve his mood at having to be in this town.

"As an opening line that totally worked." he said, his eyes skimmed over her body. "And the rest works just as well."

He smiled.

The dismay on her face was hilarious. And the beer foam around her delectable mouth was tempting. He leaned forward, thinking to lick it off and be equally forward as she had been, his body already missing the intent of her roving hand, but she backed away a step, her eyes huge and round. He caught his beer as it slid from her fingers without too much spillage.

"I…um…" She couldn't seem to form the right words, but he got it.

She thought he was someone else. Weird. Someone at the hardware store had called him a different name and then had apologized.

"I'm sorry…" she whispered, her breath coming in little gasps. "I…thought…"

She was pale as a ghost and he wondered if she'd pass out. He'd never seen a woman pass out so didn't know what to expect, but she didn't look good.

She continued to move away from him, step-by-backwards-step, her face a confusing mix of shock and fear. So she thought he was someone else. Big fucking deal. But she looked utterly spooked. He hadn't touched her, had he? Her mouth was temptingly sexy, but he hadn't really licked it. Right? That was more his brother Kane's behavior. She'd touched him like she owned him, not the other way around, right?

"Hey, relax. No harm done." He grinned.

He didn't smile a lot but ladies said he killed when he made the effort, so he did.

Made it worse. She stumbled, turned, ran.

*Shit.*

What to do? Let her go? But she could get hurt. Run into the street or something. This wasn't Bozeman or Billings with traffic, but she definitely shouldn't drive till she settled down. But he didn't even know her name. How would he calm her down? And he didn't think chasing a freaked-out woman down Main Street was what his mother meant by "keep a low profile."

Luke took another sip of beer, pondering, then almost as if he could hear his mother's insistent voice ordering him around and telling him how to treat and not treat a woman, he got up off the barstool and headed to the door. He just wanted to make sure she wasn't hyperventilating or whatever freaked-out women did.

"Baby, did some dumb ass cowboy touch you?"

He heard a deep voice demand as his hand hit the handle and pushed. He barely heard the woman's murmur, but the "Fuck that!" was loud and clear as the saloon's doors were shoved open in his face.

"Whoa." Luke dodged through the opening with reflexes honed by years of riding eighteen hundred pounds of honed, pissed off bull muscle determined to toss him off. He barely had time to notice the blonde, arms wrapped around her thin body, standing on the middle of the sidewalk, staring at the rude idiot with the jarhead haircut, who'd practically mowed him over.

He wondered if that jerk had hurt her. "Lady, are you okay?"

The words were barely out of his mouth before he was slammed against Grey's Saloon's doors, which yielded. He stumbled back inside and went down hard but popped back up, throwing the first punch by instinct, feeling his fist connect even though he didn't get a chance to focus on his target, who hit back hard, but Luke was so jacked up he didn't feel it. He'd never been in a bar fight but had broken up a lot over his years on the circuit so he was skilled at ducking and restraining, but this was a whole different game. The surge of adrenalin and power and instinctual drive was as unexpected as the sheer joy that coursed through him as he cut loose his self-restraint for the first time in his life and let everything that usually lay coiled uneasily inside him fly.

It was like slamming fists into a large oak, but Luke got a couple more solids in before his legs were swept out from under him by something pointed and hard, and he fell back. His arms were wrapped around his opponent's shoulders, so they couldn't break his fall, and he dragged the fighter with him. Pancaked, all his air whooshed out, leaving him sucking and heaving like a damned caught trout.

"Luka Aleixo Wilder! I'm not even late, and this is how you introduce yourself to your hometown?"

Marietta was nothing to him. Not a hometown. Never

would be, but he was too busy coughing and, as he tried to suck in something resembling air, he looked up into the very angry face of his mother standing over him, hands on her narrow hips like he was nine-years-old again, fighting with his half brother, Kane.

"I did not raise you to act like a thug. This is not LA." She hissed, and Luke wondered why she'd chosen that city as the hot bed of street thugs, but like everything else about his mother, her choice of similes, metaphors, analogies, and men remained a mystery.

His ankle throbbed and he saw she wore glittering turquoise boots inlaid with feathers and a bunch of other sparkling things that hurt his eyes, and the boots were as pointy as a blade. Had she kicked him to knock him down? Him. Not the other guy who'd started the whole damn thing.

*Typical.*

"Get up, Luke," she demanded.

Hard to do when pinned by a solid mass. He'd been thrown and rolled on by broncos that seemed less dense.

"This is not a fight cage. Up."

His opponent rolled off him and popped to his feet, eyeing his mother with such cool disinterest it was spooky and Luke felt a twinge of worry for her safety so he tried in earnest to sit up, but the sharp pain in his ribs was a bitch. The bartender loomed over him, his narrowed eyes and tense face looked grimmer than when Luke had walked in. Understandable as was the order.

"Don't want to see you boys back."

"Unbelievable." He heard his mother huff.

"Sorry, Talon," the bartender said to the blonde who was feathering her fingers down Luke's opponent's arm soothingly.

For some reason, that too burned.

The bartender offered his hand to pull him to his feet. Easier to do if he could breathe. His ears rang, the left side of his face seemed to pulse with his heartbeat, and the left side of his ribs screamed. Topping off that list, his lungs felt flat. The adrenalin that had fueled his response had ebbed. He took the hand and got up, wiping at his face, a little dazed when his hand came away bloody.

"Your face. You can't go out to the ranch looking like that. He'll think you're just like your—" His mom broke off, but Luke tuned her out, just like he did every time she railed about the father he couldn't remember.

He'd changed his last name to his mother's maiden name so there'd be no more reminders and no more rodeo old-timers recognizing the last name and wanting to regale him with tails of his deadbeat, hard-drinking, womanizing, fists flying, magic on the back of a bull, goddamn horse whisperer father.

Fuck him and fuck his mom for ever bringing up Helidoro Aleixo De Silva when he wasn't perfect. Today's transgression had not been Luke's fault, yet if it got him off the hook for being her errand boy spy, fanfuckingtastic.

The leggy blonde handed him a bandana she'd dipped in ice water. He wiped his face with it, blinking to try to clear his vision. Now that he was no longer swinging, his body started to pipe up with a rash of complaints, some still grumbling from the last rodeo.

*Shut up.*

"Colt." He heard the blonde whisper. "It's her. The woman I told you about who was interested in the necklace you gave me. The one at the diner the other day before you came home."

His mother stopped speaking abruptly. Silence. If he didn't count the atonal ringing in his ears. The bartender still glowered at them.

The bar was silent. Luke wiped at his face again, wincing, wondering if he'd be too much of a pansy if he got some ice for the cut above his eye, but he had to compete Saturday and vision was pretty vital, and the cut seemed to be swelling exponentially.

"Luke." His mother sounded reverent and, when he looked at her, surprised at her unusual tone since she was usually bitching about something, she looked so beautiful it hurt. She glowed, her lips parted, and her eyes shone. "I've found him. Finally. My son."

"What?" He and the other man both barked.

She reached out a slim hand toward the stranger, who leaned away from her, his face stiff, unreadable and not bleeding, Luke noticed resentfully. The blonde linked her fingers through the other guy's. She looked frozen by surprise. It was like a really stupid soap opera with really bad actors, and dramatically cheesy camera cuts. He so wanted to get the fuck out of here.

"Your brother," his mother said, "my first baby boy."

# Chapter One

TANNER MCTAVISH SHOVELED more sawdust into the trailer and spread it around. Through the bandana covering her mouth she sang an upbeat, slightly jazzy style of the Dixie Chick's "Traveling Soldier" and swung her hips in time as she spread the sawdust and then, pretending the rake were a dance partner, she danced a two-step with it down the trailer gate, slamming the handle down in time with her feet, loving the rhythmic clack, clack, clack.

She dropped the rake with a clatter.

A cowboy leaned against a black truck. Black T-shirt that fit like a dream over a cut torso, worn jeans that ended in dusty, black cowboy boots. Black Stetson tipped low, but she could see the square-cut jaw, high cheekbones, and a mouth that twisted in amusement. Fine. He caught her dancing by herself, like he could have caught her dancing any other way. So what? La-di-da. This was her ranch and she hadn't invited him unless… her heart flipped.

She recognized the stance, cocky and deceptively relaxed, and "I got the whole world in my hand and you are…?"

Luke Wilder. All-around cowboy. He was wasting his time on the rodeo circuit. He should be the international model for Wranglers. And Stetsons. And T-shirts. And probably underwear. Boxers? Briefs? Commando?

How many times had she played the game with him in her head while she stood against a cold, concrete wall while her insides heated just watching him climb over the metal bars of the chute and mount one of her bulls? Lucky bull. The desire to still know, boxers or briefs, pinched hard and low in her stomach, and she gave herself permission to stare. She worked with cowboys daily at her ranch and when she traveled with her bulls to rodeos. But he was spectacular. Luke Wilder. Even his name was doable. She'd seen him before at several of the Mountain circuit rodeos. The most handsome man she'd ever laid eyes on. He hadn't noticed her. Ever. Not once. Even when he walked past. And the time they'd been introduced his eyes had passed over her so casually and his "hello" had been so low she would have rather been ignored. At least then she could have held on to her untainted fantasies.

But he was looking today and this close he dried her mouth and fried her brain.

She picked up the rake, pretending that six-foot of muscled masculine beauty dropped in unannounced all the time.

"You startled me," she stated.

"Habit today."

She walked a little closer, forced her body to stay relaxed, and kept her breathing even, exactly like she'd enter a pen to look at a new bronco or bull. He tipped his hat back a bit. Wow, he looked a lot like her friend Talon's boyfriend, Colt. No wonder Talon had been so blissed out the three weeks they'd been together. Talon had texted her yesterday to say Colt had come back. That he was done with the army and moving back to Marietta and in with her and her son Parker and that Colt wanted to get married. Tanner wasn't surprised Colt was going all in with Talon. He was the most intense guy she'd ever laid eyes on, but Luke Wilder, this close up, had his own intense thing going on, and it was totally raising hell with her body and forget about her brain helping her out. It had shorted out at the first sight of the deceptively relaxed pose he struck.

How did Talon manage to do normal everyday things like fry an egg for Parker's breakfast, study for an exam, or go to work? If Tanner could have Luke Wilder under her and above her and wrap her legs around all of his masculine heat and power and feel him pumping hard into her, she wouldn't be able to remember her name, much less be sentient enough to text a friend to let her know that God's perfect example of a dream man had arrived on her doorstep.

Ugh. Had she just thought that? That Luke Wilder was the man of her dreams? Even as a dream man he was out of her fantasy league. Her dreams needed to chill and scale back on the ambition. Keep those lofty goals for her professional world.

God, she loved how his body looked so relaxed and yet radiated such coiled, ready-for-anything masculine energy. He looked primed for action.

Unfortunately not the type she wished she could have with him. Cowboys like Luke, who exhaled sexuality and testosterone, had so many hookup offers from buckle bunnies during their weekend rodeos that he hadn't noticed a mere mortal like herself for a lot of reasons. Luke Wilder had a lot of buckles. And a lot of fans.

And now that Luke was a part-time rep for the IBR, the International Bull Riding circuit, he'd be traveling to different ranches throughout the state during the week. Staying in different towns with different motels and different bars and a whole lot of the same sexual opportunities the rodeos offered. Tanner was not standing in any man's line. Nor would she be a forgettable roll in the hay.

But Luke Wilder did make it a challenge to remember her rules.

Her ranch was her life. Her bulls were her life. Luke Wilder was one rung on her ladder of getting her bulls into the IBR. Then there'd be another rung. And another. Triple T bulls competing at the highest level, at the finals in Las Vegas. Fifty-point scoring bulls. One hundred percent bulls. That was the dream. Not Luke Wilder.

He just looked like a dream man.

But not hers. A dream man would be a forever man. A man she could talk to about her day, about her bulls, about her concerns. A man she could joke with, who would work with her on the ranch, who'd massage her lower back and legs when they ached in winter. A man who would think she walked on water. Not a man gone all the time and fielding offers from buckle bunnies on a daily basis.

"What's so funny?" he asked.

"Just thinkin'," she drawled to stall, since once again her imagination had jumped three fence posts ahead of her consciousness.

Then she smiled even wider thinking how shocked he'd be if she shared her thoughts. Would he blush?

It was then that she noticed the swelling along one perfect cheekbone. She frowned. Punching that perfection was an art crime.

"'Bout?"

"The other guy probably cut his knuckles on that pretty cheekbone of yours."

"Unfortunately not, lucky bastard."

Tanner laughed. "Win some, lose some."

"Definitely lost that one," he said ruefully, a small smile playing around his perfectly kissable, bitable mouth.

"There's always next time."

She loved his honesty and would not have thought a man so innately masculine would have it in him. The day seemed shinier and she laughed again. Life was unfair. Luke Wilder was beautiful, sexy, skilled with a bull, and a quick wit. Luke Wilder slayed the chances of mortal men.

"Luke Wilder," she said.

"Guilty." He closed the distance in a few strides, but it was enough for Tanner to notice how fluidly he moved.

One more nail in her coffin of determination to think of him in a purely professional frame of mind.

"Tanner McTavish." She stuck out her hand, and he took it, handshake firm, total business.

So there was no reason for her tummy to flip and to hold on longer than was socially acceptable. She resisted the urge to tuck her hand into her pocket as if that would somehow make the warmth and sensation of his touch last a little bit longer.

"I'd hate to see the other guy," she said.

He shrugged, self-deprecation in every line of his spectacular body. "Not my favorite introduction to a new town."

Tanner looked at him more speculatively.

"You've never been to Marietta?"

"No."

Huh. That sounded pretty final. She'd figured he was related to Sam Wilder. Not that common of a name, and Luke hadn't grown up here, but everyone in town knew Sam Wilder. He had one of the biggest spreads in the area. And he'd had a daughter who'd left town in a blazing scandal years before Tanner was born. Luke could be Sam's grandson. But maybe not.

"Let me get you some ice for that. You're competing this weekend?" She raised one eyebrow.

He nodded and she tried not to notice the strong, tanned line of his throat, and the outline of his Adam's apple. The fact it was turning her on was all kinds of wrong. Her sister Tucker would be more his type than she was. Still, no woman should be this sexually deprived at twenty-seven. And since her sexual dry spell had long ago desiccated into a drought of dust and neglect, her hormones should have shriveled to compliant silence as well.

Damned hormones. They were only useful in bulls and horses. She stalked off towards the largest barn where she kept a refrigerator stocked with antibiotics and drinks.

He kept pace beside her silently. He moved so fluidly, all long, wiry, coordinated limbs. Her heart pinched a little, so she stomped on it to shut it up.

"You're a few hours early." She told him, feeling like she was losing her authority by being so gaga around him.

But, damn, this close up he was potent, and he wasn't even trying. She'd bet he couldn't even tell what color her eyes were. His were a beautiful, caramel brown. Almost golden like an eagle's if she let her imagination party. Again, like Colt's. Tanner frowned.

"That a problem?"

"Only if you aren't willing to run over with me to the Whispering Winds Ranch. I need to pick up some of my stock as well as Sam Wilder's to take to the rodeo grounds."

"Why's some of your stock over at Wilder's?"

His question and tone were casual, but Tanner wasn't

fooled. Luke Wilder was smart. Her inclination was to deflect the question, but she wanted to do business with the IBR so she and Luke needed to play ball. *Naked.* Okay, she did not just think that.

"Bit of a favor," she said. Short. Honest.

She couldn't tell what he made of that. She was used to silent, shrewd men but, still, Luke Wilder was a challenge to read. He slowed his ground-eating stride.

Tanner bit back the urge to swear. Her limp, a constant reminder of a devastating fall during a barrel racing final when she'd been fifteen that had ended her dominance in the junior circuit of the sport. She'd moved on emotionally and had discovered a love of biology, genetics, and animal science. She was bringing her family ranch into an age of technology and financial success that it had never experienced with her father's management. So why did her limp still have to be a thing? And why, after more than ten years, wasn't she totally immune to the graceless, screaming "look at me and my flaw" of it? Her sensitivity irritated her, which made her careless.

"You and Sam Wilder related?"

His remote face shut down even tighter.

*Way to go, Tanner.* She definitely needed to leave the charm offensive to her sister, although the kind of charm Tucker would use would have nothing to do with negotiating supplying bulls to the IBR and instead supplying her sister with a certain silent, sexy cowboy in her bed until

Tucker got bored and moved on, although Tanner couldn't imagine Luke boring anyone. He seemed calm and thoughtful. Kind. Interesting with hidden depths that Tucker would never appreciate, besides his obvious assets.

And Tanner needed to start ignoring his obvious assets like ten minutes ago. Tanner deliberately hastened her steps and pulled open the massive sliding door leading to one of her barns with far more force than necessary.

"Sam Wilder can be a bit touchy," she said. "So if you've got a beef with him, I suggest you come back around three so you can see my operation."

"I got no beef."

"Good. And you're fired," she told her Australian cattle dog, Ryder, that had continually followed at Luke's heels, one blue eye and one brown eye gazing up at the cowboy adoringly.

She hadn't even barked when he'd driven up.

"Traitor," Tanner mumbled under her breath.

HE HADN'T WANTED to come to Marietta. He'd avoided the Copper Mountain Rodeo for years, apparently for good reason. He hadn't been in town more than a couple of hours and he'd freaked-out one woman, been in a bar fight, tossed on his ass and banned from the best bar in town, pissed off his mother, learned he had an older brother. His mother had never once, not one, single, solitary time intimated that she'd had another child she'd given up for adoption. What the hell? She'd been eighteen when Luke had been born. Hadn't she heard of birth control or saying no occasionally? And what kind of a jerk had his biological father been to impregnate a minor, dump her, and return a year later just to do the whole thing all over again? Damn. No way was he passing on his genes. He'd been handy with a condom since he was sixteen. With his mother and father's pattern of behavior, he could have dozens of half brothers all over the world, although his mom had told him his dad had been in prison so maybe not.

Just Kane. And now another. A full brother this time. Whoopdidoo! Worst decision ever to come to Marietta. He needed one hundred percent focus on the rodeo. The slightest distraction could get him seriously injured. And he couldn't make any errors on inking his first IBR deal on his own.

*Get your head in the game.*

Not easy when the image of his face on another man, glaring and bewildered, was branded on his memory and playing on an endless loop. His brother had left the bar without speaking, without looking back, blonde in tow, and his mother had lit into Luke, blaming him for attacking his brother. She'd been unwilling to listen to his more reasonable explanation of events, nor had she been willing to budge or quiet her voice until the bartender had picked her up and carried her out to the sidewalk. She'd cursed him out, remembering him from high school or something. God, small towns.

He was sure people had already heard about that scene all over town by now. Samara Wilder had finally returned to Marietta with her fist-fighting, rodeo cowboy son. And now another one. He hadn't even caught the bastard's name. All he knew about his brother was that he was built like a bull, was definitely a better fighter, and protective as hell over the blonde, whose hands had walked all over Luke, not the other way around.

"Here, stop acting like such a tough guy," Tanner said, handing him an ice pack. "I've seen you ride broncos and bulls so you don't have to be all brooding, testosterone-poisoned definition of masculinity. Use this."

Judging from the way her mouth had gone all narrow, her unusual, pale green eyes sparked and had gone squinty, and her arms crossed across her chest like he was going to reach out and try to pluck one of her nipples for a snack, he'd done something to piss her off. What the hell? He'd never claimed to have his brother Kane's charm with women, but he was clueless as to what he could have done to Tanner when all he wanted to do was study her stock and breeding program. But no, she wanted to bring him to the one ranch he'd wanted to avoid despite his mother's machinations. And then they could talk business.

*Fanfuckingtastic.*

# Chapter Two

"YOU'RE GOING TO need that stitched."

"I'm fine."

"Yeah, cowboy. This is not my first rodeo. I'll give you fifty-fifty that it will split open first round."

"What do I get if you're wrong?" Luke found himself rising to the challenge in her voice.

Why did she think he was such a whiny pansy he couldn't go the full eight without a kiss for a cut. Actually a kiss would do a lot to sooth his mood.

But he didn't mix business with pleasure. Ever.

"You can take me to dinner."

He stared at her, even though he'd been speculating about a kiss. This was a business visit. What kind of bet was that?

"And if I'm wrong?"

"You pay." She stared at him hard, and he felt like he was missing something. Then she shook her head and laughed. "Relax cowboy. You're safe. I wouldn't eat a corn dog with you unless it's business."

"A corn dog is business?" Now she was just being mean. Or awkwardly flirty. "I can definitely do better than that," he said easily before he could stop his instinctual comeback.

Her pupils flared, and her breath caught and a faint pink color crept across her freckled cheeks. He moved the icepack so he could see better. She had a crazy amount of freckles. Almost like Mars dust had been sprinkled on her face. He'd never seen so many freckles. They were pale and looked soft against the creamy white of her face. He'd bet she hated them. Yet they were fascinating. Like a map of constellations.

"I bet you can."

Her voice was a whisper and caught on the last word, and he looked at her more closely. Was she flirting with him or just naturally friendly? Must be friendly, and he found himself relaxing a bit. Either way, a little friendliness felt good about now and even harmless flirting was so much easier to navigate than anger and agendas and his mom's dramas. His life currently played like a telenovela plot. A bad one. One he would have turned off. And thrown the remote across the room.

"Here," she said, taking a step closer so he breathed in her soft floral scent mixed with dust, grass, sun, and animal, which teased his senses. "Let me look."

Her hands were soft and gentle as she lifted the ice pack.

"Hold on a sec." She walked over to a shelf near a tack room and pulled out a large, white metal, first aid box. She grabbed a few supplies and then went to a fridge and pulled out two bottles of water.

"Have some water," she said. "I'll lie and say you were totally a tough guy who wouldn't take anything for the pain."

"I'm fine," he said, resisting the urge to bat her hand away.

Somehow the no nonsense kindness, the care, made him feel a little strange, off balance, but it wasn't unpleasant. Just… he didn't know what to do with it. He'd always taken care of himself.

She dabbed at the wound and he felt a sting. Then she applied some ointment and paused. "I can stitch it for you," she said. "I've stitched far worse on myself and on some of our ranch hands."

"You have medical training?" he asked, thinking her schooling had been more academic than hands on.

"No, but I've gelded a lot of horses and castrated dozens of bulls."

He jumped away from her. She laughed.

"I'll pass."

Her smile lit up her eyes and spread across her face like a sunrise. She had beautiful, white teeth that gleamed against the plump pale pink of her lips.

"Coward." She taunted.

"Smart."

She stood on her tiptoes and examined his cut. He noticed she had brown flecks in the green of her eyes, almost as if her irises hadn't escaped the freckle dusting. It made her eyes seem so alive.

"She must have been very pretty and very taken," she said. "Were you at the Wolf Den?"

"Grey's," he answered. "And yeah, definitely taken, but I wasn't asking."

"Someone must have thought so."

He scowled, remembering, but then it did seem a bit funny. The woman coming on to him, or so he thought, and him responding and then trying to be chivalrous and instead getting in a fight.

"Actually," he said, "she groped me. I was just being polite when I turned around to say hi."

"Hi, huh? That was the best you could do when faced with a beautiful woman groping you?"

"Who said she was beautiful? How'd that happen? This is my story."

"Just wanting to see how creative you are."

"I can be creative." He caught her hand. "When properly motivated."

What the hell was he doing? She was applying to be an IBR stock contractor. A client. His first client. No hands.

"I've been on the road since before dawn," he said, letting her go and taking a casual step back. "I had set up my trailer and decided to head to Grey's for a burger and beer since I didn't have time to stop for breakfast."

"Hold on. Let me get my violin." She had a stopper full

of a brownish liquid.

"What's that?" he asked as she untwisted the stopper on the bottle.

"Don't be a baby. Arnica will help with the bruising and swelling. And 'hi' doesn't seem nearly exciting and scandalous enough to get you punched, so up your creative game, cowboy."

"In my story or the next time a woman gropes me and then runs off?" And for the first time that day, he began to enjoy himself.

"She groped you and then ran off? Bad plot choice. Something must be seriously wrong with her to run away from such a marvelous opportunity." Tanner carefully dripped a few drops onto his cut, and gently pressed a cotton ball to his brow to catch any stray healing liquid.

"Thanks for the sarcasm."

Tanner laughed. "Maybe I wasn't being sarcastic."

"Doubt it."

"Yeah, your ego needs a boost."

"After my mom karate kicked me flat on my ass and took sides with the other guy, who plays rougher than most bulls I've ridden, I need more than an ego boost."

"Really?" Tanner pulled away and stared.

Her eyes searched his. He found himself relaxing even more, as if it took her skepticism blended with awe to appreciate the odd humor of it.

"I want to meet your mom."

"No. That's all I need to be in the doghouse with three women."

"So you've already pissed off two women today, and now you're starting on me? Your dog house is a bit crowded," Tanner said. "And for that you should definitely take me to dinner."

Her green eyes seemed to emanate light when she was laughing at him. Gold and brown flecks mixed with the green. Was that the color hazel? It was so unusual. And her lashes were so long, pale, and curled up, no mascara. She was so natural. A true Montana cowgirl, no artifice in sight.

"You haven't won the bet yet."

"Yet."

"Yet," he agreed, his eyes dipping to her lips.

He loved the pale pink of her unglossed lips like the first promise of dawn. And the way they curved so sweetly in a smile. Tanner McTavish might be a successful rancher and a brilliant, up-and-coming geneticist with a tart, quick tongue, but she was also a kind woman. Not the one-night stand type so he'd have no trouble keeping this strictly business. For the first time today, he was glad he was in Marietta. Happy he could potentially spend some time with her on her ranch and see her again on subsequent business trips. He liked her sense of humor and her naturalness. Not the kind who'd throw herself at him and then try to follow him to the next rodeo and then the next. He was so tired of that.

"If I knew how and wouldn't lose all self-respect, I could

fawn over you and go all cloyingly girly, which might redeem your status as a manly cowboy after getting your ass kicked by your mom."

"She actually kicked my ankle, but I probably do need some positive publicity after getting barreled into by a jealous, overly protective boyfriend and kicked out of Grey's before the rodeo even starts. Not like every cowboy won't hear the story, and I had been looking forward to a beer there."

"Is that a hint?"

"That's now impossible unless you have a secret charm weapon with the bartender at Grey's."

"Ouch. My castrating bulls and gelding stallion skills did not impress."

Luke laughed.

"And no charm will work on the bartender at Grey's. It's been tried over and over and failed."

"That I can believe." He held out his hand again. "It's good to meet you, Tanner McTavish."

She looked at his hand and then in his eyes, and it was the first time he'd seen her hesitate.

Then she took his hand with hers and pumped his hand firmly. "You, too, Luke Wilder."

He unscrewed the cap on the water bottle she'd offered him and drained it, feeling like the chilled water washed away a shitty morning.

She waited for him to finish and then opened up a butterfly bandage. "Seriously, I'd rather put a couple of stitches in it. The scar will be smaller."

"I'm not that pretty."

Her sculpted lips pursed as if she would argue with him. He waited for it, but nothing came and he felt a tinge of disappointment. He had enjoyed their verbal back and forth. Most cowboys flipped shit at each other during rodeos, but it was more hit and run.

"Now my brother, we'd need to call in a Beverly Hills plastic surgeon and a media specialist to handle the crash of Twitter, The IBR website, and everything else."

"That pretty, huh?" She stood on her tiptoes and carefully placed the butterfly bandage.

"Very. Women have hyperventilated when he signs their T-shirts and bolder ones have taken the T-shirts off for him to sign after he rides, and don't get me started on flying panties."

"He's full of something that rhymes with hit to tell you those stories."

"I've seen it with my own startled but appreciative gaze."

Tanner shook her head as if disappointed in her gender, but a smile played around her lips. He loved the shape of her mouth. It was so sexy, and bare. The soft pink pout was waking up part of him that really needed to go back to sleep.

*Business.*

But his eyes strayed back to her mouth. She looked rather proper, but with the color of her hair flaming orange red, comfort with the ins and outs of farm life, and easy-banter, he had a feeling she wouldn't be so proper in all areas of her life. Her hair alone, though scraped back from her pale face and twisted into some strange type of braid, hinted at some wildness underneath. It positively glowed in the dim barn like a lick of orangish-red flame. His fingers actually flexed as if they wanted to pull out the elastic band and run through all that fiery silk.

*Business, Wilder.* Maybe he needed to kick himself instead of waiting for his mother to do it again.

"What color were the panties?" she asked.

Not helping with his business focus one bit.

"The most eye-catching I remember were bright pink with bucking broncos on them and tassels on the sides like a horses' tails.

Tanner's lips twitched and he waited for her to laugh. "Now I think you're full of something that rhymes with mitt."

"Boy scout honor."

"And here I pictured you turning away politely when a woman is overcome by fangirl crazy. I think your mother should have kicked you and your prettier brother earlier."

"It's not that she didn't try," Luke said. "And I'm sure I sometimes deserved it." He leaned forward, trying to gauge how much she'd let him tease her this early, but he really felt encouraged by her smiles, and her warm, lightly floral scent was reeling him in. "But not today, because today, the woman who groped me may have been pretty. I didn't really notice. She was blonde and, Tanner, I'm more of a…" He drew out the anticipation, wanting to see if he could make her elegantly sculpted, bare mouth break into a smile. "Red man."

She paused, her lips tightened. He inwardly winced. Back in the doghouse. He needed to leave the flirting and the charm to Kane. Tanner McTavish might talk tough, and she had a fun side, but his last comment had definitely not tweaked it. She had a purely professional, serious, medically detached air as she eyed his bandage.

"That should hold. And, cowboy, red's what they all say at first."

The way she said at first bothered him, but before he could gather his thoughts, she turned on her cowboy heel and left the barn. The hitch in her right hip was really noticeable. He silently swore.

At first? What did that mean? To hell with this. He was no one's punching bag. Not his mother's, not his maybe brother's, and definitely not Tanner McTavish's, who, if he wasn't supposed to charm, he was at least not supposed to be pissing off.

# Chapter Three

OUTSIDE TANNER GULPED in a deep breath and then another. Thank God. Air that was NOT fragrant with the scent of whatever pheromones Luke was pumping out. He smelled so good she wanted to press against him and just inhale him.

*Freak much?*

But the combination of warm male, spice, citrus, and then some magical thing made her core weep and her blood heat, so keeping her body still and her hands off him was dang near impossible. His scent, when coupled with his rolling gait and piercing, inquisitive gaze, made her achy, restless, and swoony, and she was just not the swoony type. It was like the attraction was alive, trying to burst through her skin to escape.

And now was a terrible time for her bruised and battered libido to decide to recover. Luke Wilder might have been All-around cowboy a staggering four times, but he was also working as a representative for the IBR stock brokers, and she was finally getting a chance for her beautiful bulls to get their shot at the big time and big money, which should silence her father and his critical lamentations that he had no son to carry on their ranch's legacy. She hadn't obtained her masters in genetics and animal science and started on her PhD before putting it on hold to take over the running of the ranch while her father recovered from a devastating injury on his ATV for nothing. No way any popping ovaries were going to get in her way.

She ordered herself to think of Luke through a purely professional prism. Not think of him witnessing women throwing panties or shirts at him and his supposedly prettier brother. God, what must the brother be like if Luke thought he was the hotter man? She'd probably combust just walking into a room and breathing the same air as both of them.

Usually she thought beauty and sex appeal was overrated and hid a lot of personality flaws as well as dismissing a lot of people before they even got a chance to get to know someone. So her sexual obsession with Luke was mortifying.

Luke was here to look at bulls. Not her. Business. Not sex. She wasn't her twin Tucker, who could smile at Luke and have him anyway she wanted him for the entire weekend. She was so different from Tucker in every way. *So stop looking. Stop speculating.* Great advice until she left the barn, him right beside her, which made her so aware of their differences. Him tall, lean, olive complexion, dark brown hair that curled at his nape under his Stetson, bone structure out of a GQ magazine, and her average height, boyish slimness, nada boobs, and frizzy carrottop hair, and a million freckles across her face. Then she saw her father standing at the trailer.

"Thought I heard voices," he said in his deep baritone.

Ryder ran over to her father and leaned into him. Definite traitor.

Tanner's temper built. She had this. And her father should be resting. He had definitely been pushing himself more the closer the Copper Mountain Rodeo came.

"Bruce McTavish," he said holding out his hand. "You the IBR man come to look at our stock?"

Luke shook the proffered hand. "Yes. Luke Wilder. Nate Williams, the Montana rep, is moving to home office near Denver, and he suggested I stop by seeing as I'd be in the neighborhood. Pleasure."

"You related to Sam Wilder?"

"I've never met Sam Wilder."

Definitely not a straight answer.

"Huh," Bruce McTavish looked Luke over also clearly finding that answer lacking. "You're early."

"Yes." Luke said easily. "I was—" He was cut off by Tanner.

"We've gone through all that," Tanner said, her voice not masking her impatience, but this was her show. Her bulls she was showing Luke.

"I haven't," her father said still looking at Luke and then at Tanner and, for some reason, the scrutiny reminded

Tanner when she'd been a young teen, contemplating embarking on a crazy plan with Tucker. "But I heard there was some scuffle at Grey's earlier today between that bachelor auction soldier you wasted good money on for that pretty little gal last April, and a cowboy new to town. And Samara Wilder was in the middle of it carrying on like thirty years never happened."

Tanner didn't give her curiosity time to react. "Oh, please. You sound like Carol Bingley, Dad. What? Are you on her speed dial or something?" She rolled her eyes and glared at her father. "Luke is here to look at Triple T bulls not entertain your new penchant for nosiness. In fact, I'm running him over to Sam's to load up a few of our bulls for the rodeo. Josh and I are loading another ten from the west pasture this afternoon when I get back."

Her father looked stunned and no wonder. She was totally taking Luke's side on this. Shutting her dad down in favor of a stranger, and she felt a quick stab of guilt, but she ignored it. Her dad's sudden protective instinct was long overdue and no longer welcome. Besides this was Luke Wilder. Obviously he wouldn't be interested in her except as a bull breeder, but still the fact her dad did have a spark of protectiveness was sweet.

"After the rodeo, he's going to spend a couple of days here viewing our entire operation and meeting the ranch hands. You'll get your shot at him them, but time is tight. I got bulls to ferry and he's got to prepare. He's competing this weekend. First Copper Mountain Rodeo ever."

*Oh, my God, I'm gushing.*

Tanner barely restrained clapping her hand over her mouth. Obvious much? For a moment her father didn't answer. Not that unusual. He took taciturn to new levels and had since she could remember, but what he could say in one look would take others ten minutes of conversation.

"Think you can beat Montana cowboys, son?"

"Going to do my best," Luke said neutrally.

Another fraught silence. Luke didn't fidget or break eye contact and Tanner nearly cheered though she wasn't sure why. It wasn't as if he'd come courting her. No, just her bulls. Then her father's gaze slid sideways and held hers. She held her breath but didn't budge. She wasn't twelve anymore, desperate for comfort, praise, a hug, or approval, which she never got.

"Not sure you quite know what you've got yourself into son," Bruce McTavish said, and Tanner didn't think they were talking about the rodeo anymore. "But it sure isn't gonna be private. And a word of advice from a man old before his time, there are some things tougher to stick than eight seconds on the back of a bull."

Bruce McTavish smiled and Tanner caught her breath. She hadn't seen that smile in a long while. But she had a feeling Bruce's warning carried a subtext she'd missed, but Luke hadn't because she'd heard just the slightest hitch in his breath though he hadn't stirred—God, he must be deadly at poker.

"You go ahead to Sam's, Tanner. I can show Luke here the spread," her dad said. "I did, after all, grow up here and run it until my accident a couple of years back." He gave Tanner a hard look. "I'm not six feet under yet."

Tanner's spine snapped straight. "Yet!" She repeated. "Exactly, and you are still supposed to be taking it easy. Such as resting after your physio and not getting up early. Don't think Jorge didn't tell me that you were at the stables at dawn this morning. You're supposed to be *resting*." She emphasized the last word.

"I'm fine. I'm not an invalid, and I sure as hell don't remember seein' an MD after your name."

"We're going to be late to Whispering Winds," Tanner said, lips pressed thin. No way was she leaving Luke alone with her father. Who knew what her father would tell him about their breeding plan? She knew it would be out of date. "Then Jorge and I need to do final wellness checks. You can ride around with us when we get back."

"Thanks for giving me permission to tour my own damn ranch," her father stated, drily. "I took over this ranch before you and your sister were a gleam in God's eye. I can take care of my own damned business."

Tanner walked over to a cooler and pulled out three bottles of water. She handed one to her father, kissed his cheek, and then tossed one to Luke.

"Gonna be hot today so hydrate. You want to come say

hi to Sam, Dad?"

"Hell, no. He's crankier than I am." Her father grumbled. "And I never liked him."

Tanner laughed. "You said it."

He huffed, but his eyes crinkled in the corner as he tried unsuccessfully to hide a smile. "Careful with that rig it's state of the art and…"

Tanner slammed the gate on the trailer and bolted it, her moves quick and practiced.

"I know. I researched it. I bought it. Stop worrying. Even you, Dad, don't need or use your penis to drive."

She laughed as her father shot Luke a quick, mortified look. She hopped in the truck and it roared to life. "Coming, cowboy?"

LUKE SAT BACK and watched Tanner out of the corner of his eye. She'd tossed her bright green cowgirl hat in the back of the cab and was humming to the radio, one hand slapping out a beat on the steering wheel as she drove down the long, dirt driveway. He liked how she didn't seem to adjust her persona because he was in the truck. Her hair, scraped back into a semblance of subservience, didn't seem interested in complying with her wishes. Wispy curls haloed her face, and now that he could see her hair in the light, it glowed brighter than a flame, especially when framed by the bright blue sky and mostly tan, September landscape. Her skin was so luminous.

She must have to roll around naked in sunscreen to make it through a Montana summer day. Okay, he definitely should not have thought the naked word.

"Gonna tell me what that was all about?"

"What?" Her large greenish hazel eyes sparkled with innocence.

"Why your dad couldn't show me your stock? I got no business with Sam Wilder."

"Sam's got one of the biggest spreads. The Wilder family's been ranching forever. He breeds bulls. He and my daddy have worked together off and on over the years, helping out when they need it. I'd have thought Whispering Winds would have been on your list."

Her voice held challenge, but Luke didn't take her up on it. He was still trying to figure out why, after deciding he wasn't going to attempt communication with Sam Wilder, even though his mom had demanded it, he'd still climbed in Tanner's rig. He'd lost the element of anonymity, and the stomach for another confrontation. He didn't want to be compared to the father he couldn't remember, who had taken off leaving an infant son and a broken teen age bride and had never looked back.

Love was a fickle bitch he'd never trust, and he sure as hell didn't make promises he wouldn't keep. Luke kept his hat low and his gaze on the far away horizon. He should have stayed at the Triple T ranch. Or headed back to the fair grounds. He'd have kept his focus tighter, but the way Tanner had tossed him the water, swung her long braid back over her shoulder, and climbed into the high truck as easily as she could have slid her tight ass into a sports car had tweaked his competitive streak and her taunt, "coming, cowboy," had somehow managed to sound like a dirtiest innuendo, as well as a challenge he couldn't ignore.

"You trying to put something over on the IBR?" he asked, keeping his voice light, but closely watching for her reaction.

"What? No."

Sounded genuine.

"It's just—" She broke off. Sighed. "Look. You're young. Born well after Title IX was a thing. I love my dad but he thinks a lot of old fashioned things that aggravate me."

"Like I'd drive better to Sam's because my penis has super navigational skills?"

"Does it?" Her laugh filled the cab and stole his breath.

He had never been accused of being funny, but he really wanted to make her laugh again. Much better than her wary perusal in the barn.

"Cowboy, I'd like to see that trick."

"Could be arranged," he said quickly without thinking. "But then I'd have to swear you to secrecy."

She smiled, and he noticed a faint pink colored her cheeks.

"So, the bulls. And the ranch. And your dad. And Sam

Wilder." He made himself say his grandfather's name, like it meant nothing special to him.

She hissed out a breath, and glanced at him. "I don't want to color your opinion about Sam," she said finally. "Because I can't imagine you aren't considering signing with him as well. He has carved an enormous legacy in the area. His bulls and broncos have won many awards."

Luke noticed the past tense.

"So let's stick to talking about the Triple T." She said casually. Too casually.

"So, it's true." Luke pounced. "Whispering Winds is in financial trouble."

"I didn't say **that**," she said, quickly and with emphasis. "We aren't talking about Sam. Triple T only. I don't want my dad showing you around the ranch because, well, because his health isn't what it used to be, and I've taken over more and more of the day to day operations, so I am more current…"

She tensed up and then took a deep breath as if trying to force herself to relax. "And he doesn't like that or accept that. My dad ran a good operation. Just not high tech and he had an accident a few years ago on an ATV. His recovery was…" She took another deep breath. "Challenging. So I came home from school. I was getting my PhD in animal genetics, and I've taken my knowledge and taken over the bull-breeding program and have hired new staff and am already seeing dramatic results. I'm just getting started," she said enthusiastically. "And now that my dad is better he's expecting me to act like I'm twelve again and hand over the reins only—"

The unspoken words were like oil in his mouth. Yeah, no one wanted to be cut out, deemed less than they'd been, and all rodeo cowboys faced that especially young. It took all his will to not shift uncomfortably in his seat. Tanner was smart. Perceptive. Unlike any woman he'd dealt with.

Luke looked at her more closely. A PhD. That was serious commitment, yet she made it sound like no big deal that her plans had been derailed by her father's accident, forcing her to leave school, and probably a big city for ranch life again. Hard work. Long hours. Not much pay. Everything poured back into the ranch.

"I just turned twenty-seven, but my dad still thinks that he and Jorge, who's been with us for about twenty years, know more about breeding than I do."

"Experience is a great teacher," Luke said neutrally.

"Ugh. Not you, too. Enter the twenty-first century please. There are so many breakthroughs and new techniques. What I've been able to accomplish in the three years I've been back home has been astonishing. Our athletes are ranking higher than they ever have been. Triple T bulls are in high demand on the professional rodeo circuit. At this year's rodeo in St. Paul, our bulls were saved for the finals and only three cowboys stuck the full eight. I know we are ready for the next level of bull riding. I want our top athletes to work with the top human athletes. Oh. Sorry. That didn't come out the way I meant it."

Luke looked out the window. It had come out the way it was supposed to come out. The way he'd heard it before. Over and over. 'Why you lettin' your little brother kick your ass on the IBR? When you jumpin' to the tour?'

Like his life should be about chasing after Kane. Hell, he'd done enough of that literally growing up. No way was he ever going to ride in the same circuit or tour. He wanted to be his own man. Not Kane's big brother. Hearing the comparisons. He'd had enough of the shit from his mom, teachers, coaches.

And now he might be someone else's little brother.

That sat like a lead ball in his gut.

He uncapped the water and took a deep swallow. Gave himself time to think. Time to forget the burn of her words.

"No problem," he said.

He didn't add the rest. That he was doing what he loved. That he didn't just want to ride bulls. He loved the saddle-less broncs and the roping events, He also loved the smaller towns and the stock events and the family atmosphere. The whole Americaness of the rodeo, the history, the hard work, the fairgrounds, the charm, and uniqueness of each venue. And he liked sleeping in his own bed Monday through Thursdays, but with his new job that too would change.

"I have a younger brother who rides on the IBR."

"The pretty one? Wait! Kane Wilder is your brother?"

Inwardly he sighed. He'd enjoyed talking with her, but now it would always be about Kane.

"His rep give you trouble?"

"Nothing I can't handle."

"I got a sister, a twin, nothing like me, who's a burr in my side, too."

He laughed and tapped his water bottle to hers. "To family."

*Not.*

His day continued to careen downhill the moment Tanner pulled into the Wilder ranch. She honked as she drove past the sprawling two-story log cabin style home. One man lived in there alone. Luke liked his solitude, but that pile pushed well beyond his limit. He couldn't begin to imagine his sophisticated, intelligent, urban mother growing up on a ranch, but she had. Samara Wilder had been a top barrel racer, teen beauty queen, and straight A National Honor Society Presidential scholar before she'd run off with the son of a ranch hand. His father had abandoned his mother within months of his birth and had ended up in jail for accessory to murder somewhere near Tulsa. Luke didn't remember him. Hadn't googled him. Had never wanted to meet his grandfather. He just hoped he could keep it that way. The more he thought about his mother's demand that he visit the Whispering Winds ranch on the pretense of IBR business, the more irritated he became. His professional life was his. Not hers to muck up.

Who cared if Sam was in financial trouble? Luke had money saved but not enough to buy a massive ranch. And his mom hadn't been home in thirty years or so. She couldn't expect to inherit even if she'd growled at him that blood was blood.

Tanner continued driving toward a long, low white barn where another trailer, similar to the one Tanner pulled, was parked. Tanner had barely stopped the truck before she was out and striding toward a knot of men. Luke climbed out more reluctantly, but he admired the quick, confident way she ate up the ground despite her limp. He wondered if the injury was new or old and if it still hurt. So far he'd been lucky on his bronco and bull rides. A broken collarbone, dislocated shoulder twice, and more groin pulls than he cared to remember. And yeah, busted ribs. And a wrist. Nothing major.

He'd just reached the group, and Tanner looked up from her intense conversation with a small, wiry cowboy, with a creased face that displayed the years, the sun, and the smiles. They stood in front of a corral where an amazing specimen of a bull eyed the group warily. Tanner's eyes sparkled with intelligence and interest, and her lips curved in a smile.

"Hey, Luke, I'd like you to meet—"

"You've got a helluva nerve showing up here." The voice was gravely and angry and, as far as opening lines, this one pretty much epitomized his day. "You look just like your bastard, drunk, deadbeat, criminal of a daddy."

Luke had heard a lot of insults in his life. And crap about his dad. He turned and looked at his grandfather, who looked like he sounded. Angry. Bitter. Tall. Lean. Work-hardened. Thick, black hair, coarse with grey. Pale blue eyes, almost grey, sparkling with barely restrained emotion. Expression granite, pissed off.

"Not him." Luke said.

Sam Wilder swore and spat on the ground. "I heard about your brawl at Grey's with a soldier. A man who's served our country while you've just served yourself. Blood's blood."

Just like his daughter. Luke wondered what Sam Wilder's retort would be if he knew the so called honorable soldier was also the possible spawn of the bastard drunk, deadbeat, criminal daddy.

"Yes. It is."

He held his ground. He was fifty percent Wilder. Even a man who hadn't made a name breeding champion broncos and bulls could figure that out, but, no, Sam Wilder lived alone. No daughter. No grandchildren. No future. Only his past nursed by his bitter anger and resentment.

"No De Silva will ever be welcome here." Sam took another step forward.

For what? Did he think he could taunt his grandson by blood into taking a wild swing at him?

"De Silvas are thieving, womanizing, disgusting savages."

"Name's Wilder," he said calmly ignoring the shuffling

gaze of the ranch hands.

Tanner stood beside him, and he didn't risk a look.

"You don't know me." Luke had never once been accused of ever being even slightly out of control, much less savage. "You never will."

"There's nothing for you here. Get. Off. My. Land. And tell my slut of a daughter that I'll burn this place down before I let her step on Wilder dirt again."

Tanner's breath caught in her throat.

A pale blue gaze burned into his golden brown one.

Luke stared at the man his mother had run away from as a teenager. Twice. No stretch of imagination necessary to see what had caused that rift. Unforgiving. Judging. Hateful.

"Guess the IBR is just interested in contracting with your bulls and no others in the Marietta area, Ms. McTavish," he said to the entire group and heard several harsh inhales. "Thanks for the lift though. I'll wait in your truck."

Luke settled into the truck and ignored his phone as it buzzed with message after message. He was not talking to his mother. If he'd ignored the first call he'd received in months from her, he wouldn't be in Marietta now. He wouldn't be silently burning from the public slap down from a grandfather he'd just met. His head wouldn't be throbbing from a well-placed punch from a maybe brother he'd stumbled into, who also might have cracked a couple of Luke's ribs while he was at it.

"What the hell was that all about?" Tanner swung herself

into the truck and started the engine.

"Just another day." Luke tipped his hat to her. "But I was sittin' here thinkin'"—he went all country to hide the emotions that raced through him so fast he didn't recognize himself—"I need to learn to duck fists and phone calls."

"And family," Tanner said. "Let's load up. Can't say I'm too surprised Sam's dug his hole deeper, but your well-placed verbal slap at the end shut him up good."

She grinned and held out her fist. He bumped it half-heartedly and then smiled a little as she waved her fingers and made an exploding sound.

"You just guaranteed no one else will back Sam and give you the shoved shoulder with you being the IBR rep and also with your rodeo roots. He really needs to learn to Google."

Luke felt a little better. She'd managed to lighten his mood and he didn't feel like she was going to grill him. He didn't share that he was only the temporary Montana rep. Leverage was a tool and he needed something in his toolbox after this unwieldy beast of a day. Besides, technically, the Montana territory was up for grabs, but who the hell would want it?

"You know what you need cowboy?"

"A beer and a different family?"

"I ain't proposing." She grinned. "Let's start with a sandwich, iced tea, and a couple of Ibuprofen for you."

"Best proposal ever."

"You get many?"

"Nah. But even if I did, that would still be the best."

# Chapter Four

"THAT'S AIRBORN," TANNER said, indicating the black and white bull, "and that little man is one of my favorites, Hang Time."

Luke looked at the two bulls chewing their grain mixture that Tanner had measured out with the same care and precision she'd exercised while making him two club sandwiches on toasted hoagie rolls. The sandwiches had been delicious, but sitting in Tanner's bright, clean, slightly austere kitchen and looking at the handblown glass pendant lights that had hung down over the massive island giving the kitchen a modern, artistic flare, had made the quick meal one of the most enjoyable he could remember. He hadn't been able to help himself from snagging a few more pickles before they toured one of her barns.

"Little man, my ass. He's huge."

"Gorgeous lines." Tanner defended. "Wait 'til you see him out of the chute! He launches. So do the cowboys. Should have called him rocket."

"There you go with your challenges," Luke said. "I hope

I draw him first."

"Nah." Her brownish green eyes sparkled. "I'm all set for you to make it to Sunday's championship round. Then you can draw Hang Time."

"I'll be there, hand in the air, ridin' my eight seconds like I'm on a float in the parade."

She laughed. "Oh, so now you're king of the rodeo, reclining on your golden throne," she said. "If you draw this bad boy, the only reclining you'll be doin' is on the dirt."

"Ouch." Luke laughed. "Your mama never teach you to stroke a man's ego?"

He immediately winced at the implication. He hadn't meant it sexually, but the way Tanner sucked in a quick breath made him want to kick himself.

"I'm sorry," he said quickly. "I didn't mean it like that."

"Oh." She looked a bit startled and then smiled, but it didn't reach her eyes. "No offense taken, cowboy."

But he wondered about the look, and a trickle of dread pooled low in his stomach as he realized she hadn't mentioned her mama nor had he met her when he'd met her dad. Luke's heart rate kicked up as he watched the magnificent beast, who no longer seemed interested in its feed, as it stared back at him.

His brother Kane could and would outstare any bull. He swore he could read their minds, feel what they were going to do before they did it. It was what made him a champion, one of the top riders in the world and the cocky bastard was not yet twenty-six. For Kane, the ride was a partnership. "You don't want to dominate." Kane noted one day when he wasn't even eighteen and he'd watched Luke score his first first place. "You want to participate."

That about summed up Kane's approach to life. Not one bit sorry. But today, looking at these bulls, one-on-one, in their pens, no other cowboys around bragging or analyzing, no distractions of the back stage area of the rodeo or the hum of the crowd anticipating a show of man versus beast, the announcer ginning up the spectators, cowboys getting in their zone, he found himself really looking.

The IBR was a whole different show from the rodeo. And they would want the best bulls. He was confident in his abilities to spot the traits. To smell BS when it was being flung in his direction, but what did Kane really see when he watched a bull?

Luke had seen his brother do it. More than once. It had started when Kane was still a young teen. His complete absorption. No longer his cocky, smiling brother full of confidence and good-humored teasing. His posture would change. His pale blue, almost grey-silver eyes, so like their mother's, would seem to shimmer in concentration. His focus looked mystic. His arms would move up from his sides a little like they were lighter than air, and his fingers fluttered almost like he was trying to caress the cottonwood puffs that drifted through the air each May. And Kane, always so physical and restless and talkative, singing and dancing and laughing his way through life would be absolutely still, just the rhythmic finger twitch.

"Beautiful," Luke said, no longer eyeing the bulls, but instead looking at Tanner, her pale, freckled face shining with pride.

Her gaze intelligently assessed the animals. Then she pushed her cute, green cowboy hat a bit further back on her head and as she faced him, her gaze had a hint of shyness mingled with her pride. Luke caught his breath. Tanner was so natural, so easy to talk to. She smiled at him easily, and the fact she hadn't pushed for information about his confrontation with Sam elevated her just that much higher. His life and now his drama were his own, but he wasn't used to women who didn't demand or pry.

"What now, cowboy?"

"I want to see more."

*A lot more.*

"DEX, THAT YOU?" Luke walked back to his trailer at the fairgrounds, intending to take a quick shower after he had helped Tanner and her crew load up ten bulls for the rodeo.

She was now getting them settled into their temporary homes during the event and he'd promised her a latte after she'd finished.

The suggestion had been spontaneous. He still couldn't believe he'd made it. Tanner had been surprised as much by the offer as by the fact he had an espresso machine in his trailer, but he was addicted to good coffee and his brother Kane had bought him one for Christmas, after spending a week's holiday with him fly fishing and bitching about how Luke would drive into the small town twice a day to buy a vanilla latte. He'd taken to calling him Starbuck, but Luke didn't give a shit. Every man could have a vice and coffee drinks were his.

"Thought this was your rig." Dex, a wiry cowboy with curly blonde hair all the ladies loved, came over and shook his hand. "Couldn't believe you were coming to Montana to ride with the real men. You being a mountain boy and all."

"Gotta spank your ego sometime." Luke said easily, bodychecking the younger cowboy good-naturedly.

"You're goin' down this weekend, Wilder."

"Not without a fight."

Dex laughed and pulled on some leather work gloves as he approached the hitch of his trailer.

"You need some help making camp?" Luke asked, pleased to see a familiar face. "You're early. Thought most the cowboys would be arriving tomorrow."

Dex shrugged. "I'm between jobs so stayin' at my sisters. She's got three kids under five so an early escaped seemed best."

Luke had met Dex's sister at a few rodeos over the years. She'd always been a vocal Dex fan, which was so sweet. They'd lost their parents young, and Sarah had married at eighteen and started having kids right away. Dex was two years older and had worked hard on different ranches and competed just as hard, hoping she'd go to college since she was so smart, but she'd fallen in love with a sheriff's deputy her first semester at community college and that was that.

He helped Dex get his trailer set up.

"Thanks," Dex said. "Surprised you're in Montana. Looked up your rankings. You're having your best year on the Mountain," he said, referring to the Mountain circuit.

Luke shrugged, not enjoying discussing rankings when he was doing well or poorly, which thankfully hadn't happened yet. When it did and his reflexes began to slow, he hoped he'd have the balls to get out while he could still walk and hopefully do a whole helluva lot of other things, which was why he'd started angling to be a stock rep. At twenty-eight, he was starting to see thirty, and that was always the time he thought he'd want to settle a bit more. Buy a house with some land. Breed bulls and horses.

The whole package.

Except marriage. He couldn't see himself in a long-term relationship. Watching his mother date man after man, jumping in and jumping out, always looking for something that didn't exist, railing against God that her true love had betrayed her, abandoned her. It was like she'd been broken at eighteen and he didn't want to deal with anything that volatile.

Keep it fun and casual was his motto.

"Best of luck." Dex pulled off his gloves and shook Luke's hand.

"Thanks."

"With your scores, you finally thinkin' of jumping?"

Luke hid his sigh. He was asked this every year by almost every cowboy, announcer, stock rep, rodeo clown, even flippin' bartenders. When was he going to leave the circuit? Jump to the tour? Chase his little brother's jaw-dropping record?

"No. Good as I am."

"Yeah," Dex said, his warm brown eyes searching. "'Course." He paused. Cleared his throat. "Kane's kicking ass this year. Flippin' between first and second." Dex's voice held awe.

"Yeah. He's having a hell of a year. Proud of him. Hope he stays healthy. See you 'round."

Luke ducked into his trailer and took his shower, expecting Tanner soon. He wished Dex had arrived a little later. Privacy at rodeos was hard to find, and Dex had chosen to set up right next to Luke, and had already invited him for a beer at Grey's. Twice. He wondered what Dex would say if he heard that Luke had been thrown out of a bar. Of all the cowboys Dex knew on any circuit, Luke was probably the last one anyone would suspect would be thrown out of a bar.

Kane would bust a gut when he heard. No hope of that escaping his notice.

His phone buzzed again and he ignored it, thinking it

was his mother for the three hundredth time, but then he remembered he'd given Tanner the number.

"You ready for me, cowboy?" Tanner's voice was a bit breathless, which seemed to do something weird to his chest and something more powerful down lower.

He smiled. Her voice was like a shaft of light piercing his insides. His aching ribs disappeared along with the stiffness on the side of his face from his bruise. Not good. This was supposed to be business. He was supposed to be focusing on his competitions. He was supposed to be keeping his head in the game so he could jam Sam Wilder's negative opinions about his daughter and grandson down his throat or up his ass, whichever was more convenient.

"Come on over and find out."

Okay, he needed to chill with the flirting. He was not Kane, who led women on and then rolled out of town, prize money in the bank.

"You got any fancy flavors to wow me with, cowboy?" She teased.

"I got something I think you'll like."

Tanner laughed and hung up without saying goodbye. Luke wiped his hand over his mouth. He had sounded playful like Kane. Borrowing moves from his little brother. How lame was that? He wasn't a flirt. He was a straight shooter. What he liked about Tanner was that she seemed so natural. He didn't have to hold parts of himself back or pretend to be something he wasn't.

So what had that phone flirt been about? And why had it popped out so effortlessly?

His thoughts made him restless and made the vintage Airstream trailer that Kane had tricked out before trading up and selling this rig to Luke, seem smaller than usual, but, instead of heading outside, he did a visual check of his tidy space and flipped on the latte machine, and checked his milk supplies. All unnecessary as he always stocked up before pulling into the grounds before each rodeo.

Still, fresh air couldn't hurt. He opened the door and came face-to-face with the blonde from earlier this afternoon.

# Chapter Five

TANNER TUCKED HER phone in the back pocket of her worn, dusty Wranglers, and tried to hold back her smile. Luke was business, so there was no reason for her tummy to keep flipping every time she heard his warm-honey voice. And each time she looked into his golden eyes she found it hard to breathe.

This was ridiculous. She was a scientist. A business woman. And Luke was most definitely business. When she'd quit her doctoral program to come home and help her dad with the ranch after his catastrophic injury, she'd set a goal to create a top tier breeding program for their bulls. Triple T bulls would be going to the IBR and they'd be in the first tier of competition within five years.

This was her third year in charge, and already she'd had an IBR rep tour her ranch. And she hoped the IBR rep would have the battle of his life trying to hang on for eight seconds on the back of one of her babies. She tried to ignore the burn deep in her core. She'd seen Luke Walker mount a bull and give the signal. Hand raised, like he was casually high-fiving God "I got this," for eight long, hold his breath, heart pounding seconds. It was a ballet of raw strength, will, and fury. A thing of beauty.

And now he was going to make her a latte.

Parts of her body that had been boringly dormant for years were now whoopin' it up like it was forever Friday night, when they should be shutting up and taking a long, sleeping beauty nap.

"Business." She hissed aloud to herself.

"Tanner." Jorge interrupted her stern, opposite of a pep talk. "I'm heading back to the ranch to hook up the trailer and bring more supplies. You want a ride."

"Nah, I'm good."

*But Luke could make me better.*

"Business!" She yelped.

"What?" Jorge took off his tan Stetson and wiped his sleeve across his forehead.

Oh. She'd said that out loud.

"I got business here. I'll stay. I got my gear in the truck."

Jorge looked like he'd say more but instead he nodded and headed out. Usually at least one Triple T staff member stayed the night with the bulls during any rodeo and then usually two or three during the day to help with their care. Some contractors on the IBR tour brought their own vets. She thought of her friend Talon, who was officially starting her veterinary school next week in Bozeman, might eventually be traveling with her sometime in the future. That would be fun. But not likely now that she and Colt looked to be permanent.

That was one case of when her meddling in last spring's bachelor auction had paid off big. She and a few friends had pooled more money than they could afford and had purchased a lady's choice date with bachelor number three for Talon and apparently her choice had been Colt in and out of her bed forever.

Happily ever afters did happen. Maybe even to her someday. She mentally kicked herself for the childish thought. The ranch was enough. But still, she had to admit, the little girl who used to dream of some cowboy prince of a guy coming by to sweep her off her feet hadn't entirely grown up, despite all the times the cowboy had arrived, took one look at her twin, Tucker, and switched allegiances immediately.

She walked through the stock pen aisles that were still mostly empty. Only two ranches had arrived and were unloading their crabby and skittish bulls. She waved and quickened her step not wanting to get delayed by questions about her father's health and when he'd be running the ranch again full-time or worse hear someone brag about Tucker's "phenomenal" season, which would inevitably circle 'round to Tanner's long ago accident that had abruptly and permanently "crushed her dreams of competing in the rodeo". Like she hadn't made a new life for herself long ago. Her twin Tucker usually rode the California circuit instead of Montana and, though Tanner wouldn't admit it out loud, she was grateful for the distance.

She stopped short. Talon stood outside Luke's trailer twisting her fingers together as she looked up at him. Luke looked up and relief flashed over his face.

"Tanner. Hi. Ummmm..." He looked back at Talon, clearly at a loss, almost as if Talon had arrived and asked him for some kitchen implement he'd never heard of.

"Talon, what's up?" She hurried forward.

Talon nibbled on her lip and gave Tanner a quick embrace, but Tanner could feel the tremor.

"Colt doesn't know I'm here."

Tanner stared at her friend and pondered the non sequitur. She'd only met Colt at the auction in April but couldn't imagine why he would care that Talon had gone to the fairgrounds.

Oh. She was an idiot. "You're the blonde. From the bar."

Talon blushed scarlet and color stained Luke's sharp cheeks.

"What's up?" Tanner demanded, not liking the self-consciousness of either of them.

Her bubble of happiness, which had been growing all afternoon as she'd spent time with Luke, was deflating faster than a darted fair balloon.

"I wanted to apologize," Talon said, her voice low, her gaze nervous. "Colt misunderstood. I was so... embarrassed and surprised by my mistake I couldn't get the words out right and he thought that you had grabbed me or something."

"I'll catch you later," Tanner said, feeling like she was totally intruding.

"Stay," Luke said.

"Not a dog, cowboy."

"Please."

"No, I just wanted to…" Talon bit her lip and looked gorgeously indecisive.

Tanner stifled a stab of envy. Talon was so beautiful and so unself-conscious of it and, even though she was madly in love with Colt, Luke was probably sideswiped by Talon's beauty and sex appeal.

"You shouldn't be here without…" Luke briefly closed his eyes and ran a hand through his thick, wavy hair that had Tanner totally mesmerized.

He was so sexy with no effort. None.

"Him." Luke lamely finished.

"I wanted to apologize that he hit you," Talon said. "He's very protective of me." She flushed and looked so pleased that Tanner had the urge to kick her friend to get over it.

Possession was so not an attractive trait, and it was even worse in herself as the thought of Talon groping Luke was seriously pissing Tanner off even though it had been a mistake and Talon was in love with another man.

*Hypocrite.*

Again the hand in his hair, and Tanner thought if she'd been a dog she would have pounced on him and proceeded to lick him head to toe. Her Australian shepard, Ryder, had licked Luke this afternoon and she'd been seriously envious.

Luke opened the door wide. "Come in," he said. "Both of you, please, Tanner."

Like she wouldn't.

Tanner looked around the trailer. It was very neat and spare but warm. Like the man. The first thing she noticed was the bed in the back. A red comforter with orange, red, and white throw pillows that looked simple but stylish. Not at all a trashed, traveling cowboy bachelor pad. And the bed was not a twin.

She kicked herself for noticing. And the spurt of hooray. She was sleeping in the back of her truck on an airbed and enjoying the stars not the ceiling of Luke's trailer although… she looked at the light that splashed across his bed. Did he have a… she walked back. He did. A sunroof. That opened. She could see the big, blue Montana sky. Tanner's eyes darted around and then stayed on the long, supple back of Luke who was steaming milk and the hiss was loud in the small space. Holy shit. He really did have a latte machine.

"What's up?" Tanner mouthed to Talon.

Talon avoided her eyes, and Tanner felt her heart sink.

Luke turned around and handed Tanner a foaming latte with a leaf shape on top. She stared at it in shock and then at him. The tension in his face eased and he winked.

"Hidden talents," he said, and she smiled, pleased he'd served her first, but ordering her girly emotions to chill.

Then he handed a mug to Talon and palming one in his large, lean hands he sat in the one chair in the trailer while she and Talon huddled on the one couch.

"Luke Wilder," Luke said into the silence. Finally.

Sexiest cowboy in the west if not the world Tanner wanted to say, but she couldn't pull that one off in a teasing voice, but it was getting harder and harder to think of him as off limits. Well, he was, because he was Luke Wilder, a ten plus squared or cubed at least and she was most definitely not. But she was starting to think keeping this just business was going to be her biggest challenge. If she had the opportunity to have one night with him, one night when he could be hers, she'd take it and not look back and not regret all the lonely nights that followed if she could have that memory.

Crushing on a man who didn't know she existed as a woman sucked and now that she was getting a glimpse of his personality, it was damn near impossible to bear.

Talon just stared at him, her eyes searching his face so intently that Tanner was beginning to get an uncomfortable blend of pissed off and jealous, none of which she had the right to feel.

"Talon Reese," she said. "Soon, Talon Ewing. If that's really his name."

And didn't that comment just hang in the trailer like a bad odor. Tanner sat forward, wanting to blurt out a question. Okay, at least ten of them, but this was Talon's story. And Luke's.

"Do you know each other?" Tanner ignored her own command.

Talon shook her head. "No, I just thought that he looked so much like Colt and he's in rodeo and in Marietta and I—" She stopped. "I wondered…."

Luke took a sip of his latte, obviously weighing his words.

"You understand as much as I do," he finally said, "which is nothing."

"But how could you not know about Colt? About him being adopted? About your brother?"

Tanner clapped her hand over her mouth, afraid she'd interrupt, but what the heck was going on? But she definitely shouldn't be here. This wasn't her conversation but leaving was awkward, too. Ugh.

"My mom never said she'd had another kid before me," Luke said. "Never. I grew up in Phoenix with my younger, half brother, Kane, and my mom. I knew my mom grew up on a ranch in Marietta. That her father had been really strict and controlling and that she'd rebelled. As a teenager she said she fell in love with the ranch foreman's son from Brazil. He worked the ranch in between rodeos. They ran off together when she was fifteen or sixteen shortly before she'd graduated high school. I wasn't even two before my dad cheated on her or ran off or went to prison." He shook his head, his expression darkening. "Water under the bridge."

"Can't you just call your mom?" Tanner demanded undone by Luke's aloofness.

He just sat there, staring at the floor, legs wide, elbows on his knees, and sipping his latte. Talon's obvious distress was undoing Tanner.

"And ask her about it? Get her to talk to Colt." *Duh!*

"Not really on my agenda," Luke said. "I am not dealing with family drama during a rodeo, or ever, if I can help it. I don't remember my dad. My mom didn't keep pictures. And I sure never heard squat about another brother."

"But—" Tanner broke off.

It was so not like her to interfere, but Talon was mute and desperate and Tanner had to do something, didn't she?

"But nothing. That guy clearly doesn't seem to want to know squat about me or mom right now so let's just leave him and me in peace. Let him process."

His voice was so calm. But not cold. Kind. Luke Wilder was kind. Tanner's heart thudded to her boots before kicking into a gallop. Handsome. Funny. Domesticated. Primal and talented on an animal. Hardworking and kind. He was also undone by the news, but was trying to put himself in his newly discovered bother's place. Damn.

So they sat. Talon searching Luke's face like he was a famous art painting she'd stood for hours in line to see. Luke sprawled in the chair, mug on one long, lean leg that made worn denim look exquisitely high end, letting Talon stare at him like it was normal and he was totally comfortable with it.

"You have another brother? A big family." Talon asked.

He looked around the trailer. "Yes," he said flatly. "Just the three of us."

"Colt's been alone."

He didn't respond to that and then they all took a drink at once, and Tanner wanted to laugh at how stiff and silly they were. Except she thought Luke was hurting although he didn't look like it, but there was something so studied in his relaxed posture. And the way his throat worked when he swallowed. Talon looked tense as hell. Tanner wanted to hug her, but she thought that might make it harder.

"I don't know about my dad," Luke said. "If he had more kids. If he's alive or dead."

"Did he know about Colt? Did he try to find him?"

"I don't know."

"And they don't communicate? Your mom and dad?" Talon's voice was small.

Luke flinched so slightly Tanner thought she might have imagined it, and then he was again coolly under control.

"She said he was her heroine. Her kryptonite. More beautiful than an angel. Darker than the heart of a trained assassin. More seductive on her senses than the most aged port or a pheromone-laced French perfume. He was more dangerous than a ninja trained in ancient arts. That she was more alive with him than she'd ever imagined possible and utterly lost and dead without him."

His voice sounded mocking.

"She said that? To you? To a child?" Tanner was outraged, but also totally turned on, which she didn't want to examine too closely.

She should have been totally horrified that a man could have that kind of a pull over a woman, but instead that level of desire, the want, the descent into decadent, helpless sensuality with absolute abandon shot a thrill through her body that pebbled her nipples and heated her core. Not good.

Looking at Luke, remembering the way Colt had stared at Talon the night of the auction as if he were a famished lion and she a more than willing gazelle hurtling toward him hell-bent on being utterly consumed, Luke's mom's description of the love of her life didn't seem like complete hyperbole.

"Wow." Tanner breathed.

Luke got up, pulled a bottle of whiskey out of the cupboard and, without asking permission, put a serious splash in her mug, then Talon's, and then his.

"You got serious barista skills, cowboy."

She wanted him. She felt like she could feel him from across the trailer. Taste him, smell him. He had the same charisma of his father, she thought a little wildly. Not so flagrant or flamboyant probably, but the heat and the draw was there, and she really didn't feel like fighting it.

"What else you got?" She mouthed.

He understood. She could tell from the way his eyes glittered and her body felt warm and heavy and liquid, which was not yet the whiskey talking. She wanted them to be alone. Mentally, she willed Talon to leave, even though that was rude, and Talon was her friend and obviously worried about Colt, how he was handling the news, and knowing Talon, she wanted to understand what she could do to help him.

"DO YOU REMEMBER Jenna?" Talon finally asked after taking a large gulp of the whiskey laced latte.

"Jenna?" Luke could barely tear his eyes away from Tanner.

She seemed to glow with some inner light that was heating him up when Talon's questions and hungry eyes made him feel so icy cold. She was bound to be disappointed. Hurt. Because he already knew what his maybe brother would be going through. Why had Luke been kept? Why had Kane been kept, when Colt had been discarded? Forgotten.

Hell, he was wondering now. His mom was volatile. Exacting. Beautiful. Loving. Damaged. He couldn't imagine her abandoning a child but if the baby had come before him that would have made her young, heartbreakingly young. Hell, he didn't know if he wanted the answer. It couldn't fix anything. Heal anything. And he wanted to kick his father as far down the road of never meeting as he could.

"Jenna. She had a dimple in her right cheek. And thick, glossy black hair, and a smile and laugh you could see from a mile away." Talon seemed to wake up from her stupor. "She was real pretty. You met her at the rodeo about eight years back."

Talon swiped her finger across the phone and held it up. He saw a pretty young girl with a lot of jet black hair tumbling around her shoulders with her face squished next to Talon's. They looked unbearably young and the shot looked like one they'd taken at a photo booth and then Talon had later snapped a picture to keep on her phone.

"What rodeo?" he asked, not remembering her specifically. A lot of girls waited to meet the cowboys after their rides.

Jesus, they both looked so young. But, hell, eight years ago he'd been nineteen or twenty. Far from home. New on the circuit. Lonely. Wanting to be a man. Prove himself.

"You remember her?" Talon stood up and walked closer. "I think you met her at the Copper Mountain Rodeo here in Marietta."

He let out a breath he hadn't realized he'd been holding. He should sit back down, but Talon was really making him edgy and, combined with everything else that had happened today, his body felt tight, restless, his skin too small for his bones. Itchy.

"Never been to Marietta before today."

"You'd remember a girl, right? If you slept with her?"

*Shit.*

He so knew where this was going. No. No. No. He'd never seen that girl. Where was this coming from? It was like the biggest *Punked* day ever.

Hell, yes, he'd remember. Wouldn't he? But having a relationship when he was traveling every weekend was mostly out. Hooking up at the rodeos was beyond easy and, unless the woman was a barrel racer, or working with a sponsor, he wouldn't see her again for months if not longer. And he'd never tried.

"Talon?" Tanner asked, looking at the photo.

"I thought maybe…" Her bottom lip trembled. "I don't want anything from you. I don't need it. I love Parker and Colt does, too, and he asked me to marry him, and he wants to adopt Parker."

He forced himself to breathe. Tanner made an odd sound and she'd taken Talon's coffee from her shaking hands and put it on a side table, and then she took Talon's hand in hers and squeezed.

"So?" None of that had anything to do with him, but no one answered. "Who's Parker?" He demanded.

Even as his mind spun back to all the different rodeos, the different girls. Lots with dark hair. One with red hair who'd so pissed him off he'd become practically a saint for a while and a hell of a lot more discriminating.

"Jenna and I were friends. We grew up together sort of,

in some group homes for a while. I adopted Parker when Jenna died. It's just I thought… he looks so much like Colt, that I initially thought maybe… but Colt hasn't been home to Montana for twelve years and you both look almost like twins."

"You think I'm your kid's dad?" His voice echoed in disbelief.

He shook his head. This couldn't be happening. It couldn't. He walked around the trailer like he was looking for something.

"No. No. No way. I don't know that girl." Shit, he couldn't even remember the name she'd said. "I never met her."

Talon stood up and faced him. "You can't be sure of that. You weren't sure."

"I'm sure." He said striving for conviction. He'd remember. Of course he would. He wasn't Kane. And he damn well wasn't his father. His mom and Sam's words echoed in his head. "Blood's blood."

"She doesn't look familiar." He said, trying his best to stifle the desperate edge his voice wanted to teeter on.

"She was in love."

"No one's in love after a one-night stand." Luke ran a tired hand through his hair. "No one." He would know.

God, he was tired. Bone tired.

"She kept following the Montana rodeos. Looking for her cowboy."

"It wasn't me." Her words settled him. "This is my first Montana rodeo. I've been to Missoula once with friends but didn't... ahhh..." He looked at Tanner and felt like the biggest sleaze. "I didn't meet up with any women." He hoped that was sensitive and polite enough.

Kane would have handled this so much better.

"I rode the California circuit for two years and now the Mountain State circuit for the past eight."

"Would you be willing to take a paternity test?"

He stared at her. It had to be a stunt. Or something. He kept staring at her, waiting for what he didn't know, but her eyes filled with tears. She was serious. This girl was all kinds of crazy. His maybe brother was lassoing his star to crazy town, just like his dad had.

Luke felt sick.

"Talon," Tanner said, standing up, her voice soft and slow whereas Luke felt like throwing something.

"That's a pretty big stretch and an accusation." Tanner was stroking Talon's back soothingly. "Maybe think on it a bit first, talk to Colt."

This day couldn't suck anymore. First the demand from his mom. Then the fight. Then the big reveal of some brother he'd never heard of. Then being tossed out of a bar. Tossed off his grandfather's ranch. And the grand finale—now he was being accused of fathering a child with a woman he'd never met. At least he didn't think he'd met her. And he wasn't that hard to find. He did give women his name.

Anyone could find him. Google the damned circuit. His schedule was online. Stats online. Injury status online. Earnings… that must be it.

"Money," he said flatly. "Did he send you here for money?"

"What?" Talon, who'd sat down again at Tanner's urging, jumped to her feet again. "Why would you think that?"

"Obvious conclusion."

He remembered how hard his mother had worked to get Kane's father to acknowledge him. First it was for money because she was putting herself through school and had two small boys. Then it was for pride. Then it was for Kane's feelings. His sense of security and belonging. His schooling.

"You said you'd adopted your friend's kid. That… that your… fiancé…" He would not say the word brother; it was too damn complicated and alien. "Was going to adopt him, which makes me pretty damn superfluous if I were the biological father, which I am not."

He used condoms. Always. And hadn't had any accidents.

He was not going to put some woman through what his mom had gone through. He knew from personal experience, first dreaming his dad would appear on the horizon and play happy families and then watching his mom spend hours trying through legal aid to get Kane's dad to accept his paternity and provide financial support, that the search for daddy's acceptance was a moving target. A sick game of whack-a-mole. Impossible to win. And he one he had no intention playing.

Damn it. Just damn it. The day sucked. The town sucked. Now Tanner would think he was some jerky, cavalier cowboy who rolled into town, mounted a bronc and a bull and then a woman, then sauntered off into the sunset. He'd never dodged a woman's texts or calls after he slept with them. He knew plenty of cowboys who did, but he sure wasn't one of them.

And he sure as hell wasn't going to give the town of Marietta one more reason to despise a Wilder.

"Fine," he said. "I'll take a test. But I want that so called brother of mine to get a cheek swab too. "And now"—he opened the door wide to his trailer—"out. Both of you."

He would have loved Tanner to stay. To talk to her about her bulls and her breeding plans. Hear her laugh again. But he had to get all this crap out of his head. Get himself together because he wasn't going to be maimed or killed because he was distracted, and he'd never scratched from a rodeo. Ever. He'd imagined this afternoon going so differently.

But his mood was all shot to hell along with the rapport he'd had with Tanner. Now some blonde who'd mistaken him for someone else was going to drag his reputation through the mud. Just another Wilder who couldn't keep it in his pants. Whatever happened to innocent until proven guilty?

Hell, the Kardashians had less drama. Tanner stared at him and he had no idea what was going through that agile mind of hers, but he felt like a bug pinned to a slide the way she was eyeing him.

Tanner drained her coffee mug, washed it out in the sink, and deliberately full body brushed by him.

"Thanks for the whiskey and splash of coffee, cowboy. See you around."

# Chapter Six

TANNER ROLLED OUT her thick, self-inflating air mattress in the back of her truck and spread out her favorite comforter as well as her sleeping bag as the September evenings and early mornings could get chilly in Marietta. Although, so far, it was still fairly warm. She stretched out, eyeing the constellations, but she still couldn't settle.

Her attraction to Luke Wilder. Her hope of signing a deal with the IBR now played alongside the possibility that Talon's fiancé, the former bachelor/army special forces sniper, was Luke's brother and that Luke might be an unwitting dad. But over all of the voices, the clashing words and fears and hopes, was the undeniable attraction she felt towards Luke and the wondering if he could possibly be attracted to her, not just to talk to and work with but more.

If it had just been physical, she could have acted on it, or let it go. She hadn't had a relationship since she'd moved home over three years ago. She'd never mastered Tucker's enthusiastic embrace of the one-night or weekend stand.

"There's only one of me, and so many smokin' hot cowboys lining up." Tucker would always joke and toss her long, smooth auburn hair over her shoulder like none of the men really mattered, except for how their desire and attention thrilled her in the moment.

Tucker loved the attention and the chase. Once caught the cowboy bored her.

Tanner wished she could channel at least some of that. She was lonely. No matter how much she loved her ranch and her bulls and her science, she couldn't stave off the growing hole of emptiness that clawed at her some days. Seeing Talon connect with Colt in April when Tanner had impulsively talked four friends into pooling some serious cash to bid on the soldier bachelor number three, had broken something open inside of her. Talon too had been lonely, and she'd jumped fearlessly into what she'd been told seriously by Colt wouldn't be more than a two or three week fling together because he had to head out on another deployment, and yet he'd come back after completing his time. He'd proposed marriage. Was going to adopt Parker. It was like a movie.

Talon's happiness was inspiring, but Tanner didn't know if she could be so fearless. Could she jump into something with Luke just to watch him drive off Monday night after spending the day at her ranch after the rodeo with no guarantee he'd drive back again? Luke was at the top of his game in the rodeo. Barring injury, she crossed her feet and fingers and wished hard for his safety, he could compete another five or more years and easily be competitive. And his job involved a lot of traveling.

She had a ranch and a business. She traveled too because a team always went with the Triple T bulls to rodeos. If she could jump enough bulls up to the IBR, maybe she and Luke would be at the same events. And if he treated her like a buckle bunny, what then? She didn't have Tucker's confidence. She didn't have Talon's resilient heart that had been battered over and over again but was still beating, whole and capable of a deep love for an orphaned boy and an intense, isolated soldier.

Deep inside where Tanner never looked or let anyone else see, she still felt like that broken fifteen year old girl, patched together enough to survive the life flight to Seattle's children's hospital where she stayed for nearly four months with no visits from her father who "couldn't leave the ranch and didn't know a dang thing about medicine," and only a handful of phones calls from him and her twin who was "too devastated to talk about it."

Tanner sat up. Not a good night. And pity parties were boring. So she wasn't the pretty twin. So she couldn't barrel race competitively. So she walked with an awkward limp. BFD. Move on. And she did. She hopped out of the bed of her truck, ignoring the sharp pain in her right hip and pulled a clean, flannel, western shirt from her duffle bag.

She'd check on her bulls before sleeping. There was always work to do that would turn her mind off and tire her body enough so when she hit her mattress, whether it was her bed at home or in her truck, which she often preferred to the trailer as she loved the spangled sky, she'd fall into a deep, restful sleep.

She walked across the dirt and slid open the door to the large barn where the bulls were kept. She had delivered ten bulls today. Four more would come tomorrow. More than any other Montana ranch. She'd brought several of her favorites—Hang Ten, Dervish, and Slayer because she knew the IBR stock rep would be watching them compete if they got drawn. Luke would later view the videos frame by frame and compare their athleticism to other bulls both already on the IBR tour and vying for a position with the tour. He was already booked for a full day out at her ranch on Monday and he might stay through Tuesday. Almost a whole week with Luke Wilder.

She tamped down on the thrill that ran through her blood at that thought. Business. Business. Business. She chanted. No jumping him. Yeah, he was hot, but it was more than that, and that was what she was most afraid of.

Getting Triple T bulls on the IBR Tour was too important to let her hormones interfere. She would maintain professionalism. She promised herself, watching her favorite pair of green cowboy boots eat up the sawdust and dirt of the path to the bullpens. Her resolve melted the moment she saw the long, lean figure of her cowboy, one arm hooked over the railing, one boot up on a rung, posture relaxed but shoulders rigid and the contrast of tension was for some complicated reason so sexy. In his other hand loosely dangled a bottle of beer that was full.

On complete impulse, which was far more like something Tucker would do, Tanner reached out, snagged the bottle and took a deep swallow, very conscious of his gaze on her.

"Thanks, cowboy. I was thirsty."

Unable to let that slightly suggestive action and comment hang alone in the space between them, which would declare her interest as clearly as a dating site, she rushed on. "He's a beauty, huh?" She stared at Hang Ten. "I have four bulls that maintain a one hundred percent rating this year."

"Beautiful." The deep timber of his quiet comment settled deep in her stomach, curled around her spine, and crept lower.

She didn't want to read anything into his voice or his one word response but, damn, the way he looked in the dim light of the bull pen area made it dang near impossible not to envision every sexual fantasy she'd stomped down since the first moment she'd seen Luke Wilder three years ago at the Steamboat Springs Rodeo.

She swallowed hard and handed back the beer bottle, not able to hide the shake in her hand. She shouldn't have acted so impulsively. What must he be going through, meeting his secret brother, getting kicked off his grandfather's land?

He took the beer. "Do you know this is the second time

a woman swiped my beer today?"

Her breath fractured. Blood surged to her cheeks. No way to hide the fierce embarrassed blush. She was such a clumsy, girlish cliché. She was a scientist. A business owner. Goal oriented. She needed to get a grip.

"Only this time," he said softly. "I don't mind."

He brought the bottle to his mouth, took a long swallow before holding it out to her.

Tanner was more a whiskey girl, but beer had never tasted so amazing. It slid like nectar down her throat and she felt as if the taste fizzed and danced on her lips and tongue. She drank, feeling like she was in high school again, and then handed it back feeling silly and turned on simultaneously.

He smiled and took another swallow. She'd only seen him a smile a few times, but this time, his entire face, his entire body smiled. Deadly. There was no way she could resist that. And the way his gold-brown eyes had heated like honey as they drifted over her face killed. Beer back to her.

She tilted the bottle to her lips, but before she could swallow a shiver started deep in her body, radiating out, and it was almost like the earth was shaking. Her heart and blood rushed and instinctively she reached out and put her hand on his waist. Heat. Solid muscle. Her fingers curved, gripped, and she took a step forward, unable to resist his draw.

His golden eyes flared, and it was like a match had been lit, and she so wanted to close the rest of the distance between them. A millimeter was too much of a chasm. She wanted to feel him, all his heat and hardness and strength and sheer male energy. His hand snaked around the back of her head and cupped it. She looked up. His eyes searched hers, questioning, but hell if she had any answers. She shouldn't do this. Not smart or professional and it would be hell on her ego and heart if he didn't kiss her and, worse, when he stopped, but if she didn't go for it, she'd regret it. Big time. They stood there. She, feeling like time had slowed, every second fraught with suspense and he, who knew what was going on in his mind, but women probably threw themselves at him daily, and Tanner couldn't quite bring herself to care.

All her good, business only intentions were ground into the dirt under her boots. No way would she ever say no to Luke Wilder. It was like all the times she'd seen him, watched him, admired him, as she tried to ignore him, all condensed into this moment, this one opportunity.

"You gonna stand there all night thinking about it, cowboy?" Somehow she found her voice and taunted him. Maybe if she pretended this wasn't the most exciting and scary moment of her life she'd believe it, too. "I thought bull riders were fast."

She so did not just say that! She should pull away, mortified, but the way his eyes searched her face as if he was looking into her soul kept her rooted. She felt like he was seeing her, really seeing her. The woman and the businesswoman. The scientist and the rancher and the lonely woman who sometimes felt insecure.

His hand continued to cup the back of her head, and the other came up and his thumb lightly stroked the angled, determined line of her jaw while his fingers feathered along her cheekbones.

"Only on the back of a bull or bronc, cowgirl." His voice teased her nerves which all seemed to be standing up on alert. "For everything else, I like to take my time."

*Oh, my God, you are so perfect.*

He smiled, which flipped her heart. "I think today you had a front row seat to many of my imperfections."

"Did I say that out loud?" Again the blush surged across her cheeks. "You are supposed to be polite and not call attention to those things."

"Where's the fun in that?"

"I can be fun," she whispered, knowing she was practically shoving herself like a laden platter into his hands.

*Take me please.*

His fingers speared through her braid and, before she could protest, they trailed through her hair. His gaze was hooded, focused on her tight curls that sprang through his fingers.

"It's like fire," he said softly.

Her mouth burned and she ached for him to touch her. Her hair might be the color of fire but to her it was uncontrolled frizz and the fact he was staring at it while it slid through his fingers astonished her.

"Luke." She was uncertain.

He bent his head and her lips parted. She felt the first whisper of his lips along hers. She bit back a moan, dropped the beer bottle on the ground, and took another step forward until her body was flush with his. His mouth traveled down her neck and Tanner shivered and clutched his arms. His biceps felt like stone hewn from Copper Mountain and desire punched her low and hot in her gut, almost like a brand.

He had to really kiss her. Had to. The desire like a drum thrummed through her body. Instead, his hands trailed fire as they slid down her arms and anchored on her hips. But instead of a full-body press, which she craved, he used his hands to create a small amount of distance, which she hated.

"Tanner." He breathed against her lips, his brushing hers, setting her body ablaze. The light brush of his mouth was pleasure personified and torture because she craved more, needed a dark, hungry kiss. "What are you doing to me?"

THAT WAS ALL the permission she was going to get, so she stood on tiptoes, curled her fingers in his dark brown wavy hair, and pressed her lips against his, first softly then hungrier. She sighed into his mouth and all of her worries about her father, getting an IBR contract, her blossoming feelings towards Luke, faded away under the sensual assault as she slid her tongue along the seam of his lips and felt his heart accelerate and slam against hers.

His fingers played with her hair, touched her cheeks, and slid down her body to rest lightly on her waist. It was beautiful, but it wasn't enough. It was as if she'd been parched and now offered a cool drink of water. She wanted the entire glass and then to chase it with a bottle of champagne and hang her head out the window of a speeding car and shout at the moon.

He whispered her name and that only inflamed her more. She stepped into his body, rejoicing when she could feel him hard against her stomach and she rubbed against him, revering his heat and length and response. It had been so long for her. And she was touching him. She wanted more. His shirt off. She needed to feel his skin. She wasn't even aware she'd started unbuttoning his shirt until he caught her fingers.

"Tanner," he murmured against her mouth.

She kissed him. Stroked her tongue along his lips.

"Cowboy." She smiled up at him and realized he was clasping both of her hands, which had been marauding all over his body like she had total rights to him.

"Sorry," she whispered, hating how the words caught in her throat.

But if she were going to be brave enough to act on one of her long running fantasies, she had to be brave enough to suck up the consequences. Only she wasn't really sure how to explain why she'd jumped him. The truth would probably send him packing back to the Denver area.

"I'm a little out of practice."

That had *not* been what she'd intended to say.

His quick smile, the warmth in his eyes, nearly melted her at his feet.

"I'm sure you're just teasing this cowboy," he said in an "aw, shucks" way that made her want to wrap her legs around his waist and show him that, no, she was totally serious and completely dedicated to getting experience pronto. "But it's not a race."

She nibbled on her lower lip. So he wasn't opposed to kissing her, just she was going to fast? That was a role reversal she'd never heard of and her stomach sank. Just too fast with him, she translated. From the lines of buckle bunnies she'd seen over the years waiting for his "autograph," slow was not his operative word.

He cupped her cheeks, his thumbs smoothing across her cheekbones.

"Trying to do the right thing here, Tanner," he said softly.

"Don't."

"You could try to help me out." He suggested softly.

"You are ruining the reputation of rodeo cowboys everywhere," she said, striving to keep her voice light like she hadn't been turned down or that she had but didn't care. "They are weeping."

She pulled away, trying to be a good sport about it. The spell was broken. Her impulse had played out and she was more than a little embarrassed she'd been swept away and he had been holding back. She'd been the one who'd been the designated driver during nights out. She'd been the one to pull her girlfriends out of the arms of random cowboys they'd picked up in bars. She'd always been the good girl, coming home to study, while Tucker and her friends had lived it up.

She signed and smoothed his shirt.

"You're safe, cowboy. I'm back in girl scout mode."

"You don't need to go that far," he said. "I just—" He took a deep breath and ran his hand through his thick hair, which made her twist her hands behind her back to curb any crazy impulse. "It's just been a helluva day."

Tanner wanted to kick herself. Of course. Finding out he might have a brother. Having his grandfather, whom he'd never met, throw him off his ranch so publically and then Talon's accusation. No wonder he was reeling. He needed a friend or at least a business associate to help ground him, not some woman jumping him.

"Yeah," she said, starting to quickly re-braid her hair. "Tough day."

He covered her hand that was quickly reweaving her hair.

And just like that time, stopped for her and she was falling into a vat of melted chocolate caramel. His touch was like a brand. She felt it to her bones.

"Your hair is lovely," he said.

It wasn't. She knew that. Her hair had been a source of teasing at school and an irritation her entire life.

"And we may be working together," he said carefully. "And I wouldn't want…"

"Yes," she said, wishing a few sips of beer could explain her uncharacteristic behavior.

Why had she thought she could pull a Tucker move anyway? The disappointment and embarrassment made it hard to breathe, but he didn't have to know that.

She hoped, probably unrealistically, he wasn't embarrassed by her dumb-girl move. Ugh! What if he pitied her? Desperate small-town cowgirl. She dragged out a smile and the chipper voice she'd developed all those lonely and scary days in the hospital so many years ago. He probably thought her biological clock was ticking. Well, it wasn't.

"You're right, of course." She pinched her thigh hard to concentrate on that pain instead of the other that was making her feel like somebody was pouring ice cold water in her body, filling her up. "Not sure what got into me, but I'm sure I'm not the only cowgirl to jump ahead." Her smile felt like it was going to crack along with her face. "I'll um…" What to say now? How to walk away back to her truck? "See you around."

"Let me walk you back to your rig. Where'd you park?"

"I'm in my truck. I love sleeping under the stars and I'm

a big girl. I can walk back alone."

"I know, but I'm traditional so the cowboy in me won't allow that. Besides my mom already kicked my ass once today. Don't need a repeat."

She smiled, but somewhere deep inside felt a pang. She could so fall in love with this man. He was kind. And beautiful. And sexy. And smart. The perfect cowboy and so out of reach he might as well be on another planet. There was no way she could walk through the night with him. It would be like standing too close to a flame.

"Actually, I came to check on my bulls."

But that didn't drive him away. Instead, he stayed with her while she checked on each one, talking to them, making sure their bedding was adequate and that they were comfortable. Most were sleeping and not in the mood to greet her. She headed with Luke toward the exit.

He smoothed his hand through her hair. "Your hair is as soft as I imagined. It's like a beautiful sunset-colored halo," he said, his eyes searching as if trying to absorb the vision, the screaming color.

Tanner caught her breath at the look in his eye. She didn't think anyone had ever before looked at her like that, like he was really seeing her, cataloging all the things he liked. She was used to men noticing only her sister, then liking her later, after they realized she was funny and smart. Career-oriented.

She caught his hand. She could be mature about this.

Take what she could get. "Okay, walk me back, cowboy."

They walked outside. The air was definitely a bit damper, chillier.

"You want to stay in my trailer?" He offered. "I can sleep in your truck."

"No, I'm good," she said. "The weather's cooperating. I've got flannel and sweats and a sleeping bag."

"That sounds romantic." He commented.

She laughed. "That's how I roll. I'm beatin' 'em off with a stick."

"Nah." He laughed. "I'm thinkin' you probably need a club and a couple of bouncers."

The playful light in his eye, combined with his quick reply, and gaze narrowed on of all things, her hair, zinged heat through her, and Tanner realized she spent her whole life so caught up in her dad's opinion of beautiful—Tucker, Tucker, and Tucker, which had been a one-two punch with Tucker's sparkling and sky-high confidence and string of romantic conquests that Tanner continually sold herself short.

"Left my bouncers at home," she said softly, a little shy as she bodychecked him, unable to resist the lure of his warm, wiry strength. Friends. Maybe they could be friends. That was something. Better than nothing.

It felt so natural walking with him like this, touching him, yet she'd only met him today. She'd seen him before, more than a few times, and had stared and longed and fantasized and tried to ignore, but today was the first time she'd said his name aloud. Looked into his golden eyes. Been able to talk to him.

He stopped, turned to her, and his tanned, calloused hands cupped her face. He bent toward her, his head blocked out the moon, and his lips teased hers apart, kissed her briefly then he rested his forehead against hers. Their breath mingled and, even though Tanner had kissed more than a few men, and had definitely not been celibate in college or grad school, nothing she had ever done with anyone before had felt as intimate.

"Hell of a day." She breathed, echoing him and reminding herself not to read too much into his gesture.

"One of my worst," he admitted, surprising her with his honesty.

Cowboys were tough. Uncommunicative. But Luke Wilder… she bit down on her lip as a deep longing welled up. She liked him. Really liked him and the want and like clamored louder. It had whispered along her spine before during the times she'd watched him behind the scenes at a few rodeos, watched him calf-rope, saddleless bronco ride, bull ride, but now the want banged. Shouted. Insisted.

And she didn't quite know how to silence it.

"But definitely an upside." His thumbs were warm against her skin as they drew circles on her cheekbones.

"Yeah?" It took all her effort to not lean into one of his hands, kiss his palm, his fingers. "I'm better than a bar fight with an out of the blue mystery brother? And getting tossed out on your ass from your granddaddy's ranch on the day you met him. Then there's the paternity suit. Better than that?"

He laughed as she meant him to, and despite the longing, despite her earlier embarrassment, she would get through this. She'd work with Luke Wilder. Admire him at arm's length and get over it. She'd have to.

"Okay." She tried to sound businesslike about it, act natural, even though she wasn't. She felt stiff and awkward and prickly like she was being poked over and over. "Umm..." And then, despite all her promises to herself, tears pricked her eyes, which was just plain stupid.

But she'd made a mistake with him and now things were going to be awkward between them, whereas before they'd been warm and fun and she'd felt for the first time in a long time not so alone and she'd trashed that. She felt like, at long last, she was out of her awkward phase and that she could find a man she liked and was attracted to who would like her back and not be disappointed with her looks, especially when he met her sister. Stupid fantasy.

And what if she'd ruined her chances with the IBR because he wouldn't want to deal with her? She had to save this fast and making herself scarce was probably her best option.

"See you on a bull, cowboy, or on your ass." That had the right amount of cheekiness but would have sounded better if her voice hadn't broken before she could get the last word out.

She spun quickly and strode away, one hand raised, a little finger-wiggling like she'd seen other women who were cooler than she was do.

"Tanner, wait." His quick stride easily ate up the distance even though she didn't stop moving.

His hands slid down her body and rested on her waist.

"Talk to me," he said, his voice low in her ear and reverberating down her spine. "What's wrong? What happened?"

"Nothing."

She so wanted to lean back against him, savor his hands at her waist. Pretend.

"Tanner, tell me. This day has been one of my worst, but meeting you has been the best part. Best in a long, long while."

She turned around, searched his beautiful caramel gaze.

"I'm glad," she said softly barely stifling her incredulous "really?" in her mouth. She would like to make him happy. "Me, too," she said. And it was the truth. "I just made it awkward, and I'm so, so sorry."

"You haven't made anything awkward. It's just"—he heaved a sigh, released her, and took a step back—"it's just me."

She'd heard that before. She knew the game. That meant it was her.

"I just started this new job, and I'm in the process of having to move and something's going on with my mom that she still hasn't explained and that was before all the crap today. I'm in to no position to…"

"I ain't proposing, cowboy," Tanner said.

"I'm being an ass."

"No," she said, unable to stop herself from letting her fingers play along the chorded muscles of his upper back before she speared them in his thick, wavy hair that grew back from his forehead.

"You are making this really, really hard for me to behave."

"I don't think I want you to behave," she confessed. "But I know you want to."

"Tanner…" He caught her fingers and pressed them to his lips, kissing one after the other.

Her breath was ragged and mingled with his.

"I really like you," he said huskily, but it was like an ice cube slid down her shirt. "I want to spend more time with you, but we might be working together."

"So," she challenged, not sure why she was pushing when she'd been trying to keep it business from the start. "If I only kissed guys I wasn't working with in some capacity, I'd never be kissed."

She tried to pull away, but his hands still held hers, his eyes burned.

"I don't know what to make of you, Tanner McTavish," he finally said, and didn't that make two of them? "This might be one of my biggest mistakes, but it's just really bad timing."

He was right about that. Part of her wanted to smack him for being so honest and honorable and the other part wanted to hold him close, but he sure needed to stop being so perfect. She'd seen buckle bunnies lined up by his trailer for an autograph hang on him at the sponsor advertised bars after the events. Luke Wilder had rarely been without company.

"I'm not..." He seemed to search for a word. "Right tonight." He took a deep breath and stepped back, one hand running through all that luxuriant hair, making it flow back from his forehead in a graceful wave, and then his hand smoothed over his mouth. He looked at his boots, kicked the dirt a little, and then looked back at her. "In my head. My mom's got something she's brewing that I don't like or understand, and as far as my brother..." He spread his arms away from his body, fingers wide as if he could drop the burden. "Then your friend. I can't even remember her name."

"Talon."

"Yeah. And her kid. I'd never leave some girl stuck like that." He grimaced. "Like my mom was left. But I started the circuit when I was eighteen. This is my tenth year." The silence hung there, and Tanner imagined a long line of invisible women. "I don't dodge phone calls or texts, and I'm pretty easy to find so I'm sure I never knew that girl, but... shit."

Yeah that about summed it up.

Again the strong, tanned hand spearing through his hair, and Tanner found it so sexy it was all she could do to not reel him in for a true round of lip mash-up, but the heaviness in his shoulders, the shuttered look of his face hurt. She wanted him happy, playful again.

"You're a really awesome cowboy, Luke Wilder. And a better man."

He looked at her, his hair falling sideways over one of his eyes and laughed ruefully, and she could imagine him as a kid.

"I feel like a stupid prick."

She laughed. "Ouch. Can't have that. Okay, so let's start over." She stuck out her hand. "Tanner McTavish."

He shook his head, smiled, linked his fingers with hers. "Tanner McTavish. My day has sucked, but meeting you is the best part, and I would like to see you again when I'm not feeling so out of sorts. Would you please do me the honor or being my date for the steak dinner Saturday night?"

"Smooth, cowboy," Tanner said, trying but failing to stifle the thrill zinging through her at his words.

"Is that a yes?"

"Maybe." She tried not to let her gaze rove hungrily over his body, but damn the man looked like a god in Wranglers. "But I want to hedge my bets."

"How so?"

"If you draw Hang Time, you're gonna be tossed on

your ass like never before and won't be able to dance with me."

"If I draw Hang Time, I'm going to be in first place going into the finals and will feel like celebrating with a slow dance, under the stars, far away from the lights and the crowd."

"Still hedging my bets, cowboy. Go to the parade with me tomorrow. Kick off the rodeo with one of my favorite events."

He made a face. "Pretty public," he said.

"You can size up your competition. Make them tremble with fear. Besides there's funnel cake."

"And you."

"And me."

A light lit in his eyes turning them to honey. "Tanner McTavish, is there licorice at this parade?"

"Maybe."

"I love Red. Rope. Licorice." He nuzzled her ear and that sent shivers through her entire body, and somehow she got the feeling he was not planning on eating it.

*Bring it on.*

# Chapter Seven

LUKE STILL COULDN'T sleep. Not good for a man who was planning to sit astride eighteen hundred pounds of thrashing muscle, furious and determined to toss him airborne, and trample him just to drive home his point that he was pissed off in a couple of days. Luke didn't need to meditate, expose Zen principles, and imagine himself one with the bull to know he had to get his shit together or withdraw from the competition. The rodeo had always felt like home.

He'd always been able to focus. Always been able to leave the rest of the world behind when he pulled onto the rodeo grounds.

Usually it all fell away, the loneliness, money concerns, aches and pains all dissolved when he'd set up his rig, flipped shit back to other competitors, checked his equipment, shared a beer, and some stories. Tonight his mind wouldn't settle. Back to his mom's demands. Back to the fist of his brother connecting. And Luke's connecting back. The odd thrill of a fight, something he'd never done. Had deliberately eschewed, proving that unlike his father he had control. And now the dislocating sense of recognition and loss and anger and regret he couldn't quite sort through.

How the fuck did his mom lose a son? How did she go twenty-eight years without a word about it? Like her firstborn son had never happened. What else was she hiding? Did he even know her? Were any of those tight-lipped stories he'd manage to wheedle out of her as a young boy about his father even true? Had his father really walked away from him? And what was his brother, Colt, Talon had said his name was, thinking tonight?

Luke couldn't imagine it was any better than what he was thinking. What he was feeling. And Luke didn't specialize in analyzing feelings. Kane was more into the analysis. Fuck. His mom had probably gone off like a bomb to Kane since he hadn't picked up any of her calls. He didn't know where his brother was on the tour. Didn't check in ever. Kane did all the connecting. At least with four weeks on and one off, he stood pretty decent odds that Kane wouldn't be able to soothe their mom in person.

Unable to handle the curved, beige lines of the ceiling of his vintage Airstream trailer another second, he grabbed a beer from the fridge and opened the door, intending to sit on the top step and try to not think about Tanner and how he'd let her go tonight even though she'd obviously been willing, and he definitely wasn't going to think about his brother—make that brothers—now. Shit. One was hard enough to deal with.

Only when he opened the door, his brother stood at the bottom. The new one. The silent one. Luke bit back the instinctive curse, shoved the beer in his brother's hand, and ducked back inside to grab another. Awkward as hell but might as well get this over with. He pushed outside, not even realizing he was bracing for another round of whatever until his brother took two steps back, twisted the cap off the beer, flicked it with enviable precision through the open door of the trailer into the sink and then, beer dangling between two fingers, he held his arms slightly away from his sides as if daring Luke to take an open swing.

Luke blew out a breath. He might not be the man everyone else thought he should be, but he was who he was, and he wasn't by nature a fighter. He didn't have anything to prove to this guy.

"Not that I'm complaining, but I've been kicked by bulls that caused less damage than you did today," Luke said.

His brother tipped the beer to his lips, but his eyes, the same color as Luke's, he realized with a punch of dismay, never wavered. Luke felt like he was in the crosshairs of something fierce. He'd thought to pull out two chairs for them to sit, but he didn't think the man before him could relax enough to sit, and Luke doubted it was wise for him to try to get that comfortable. Defenseless. Who the hell was this guy?

"She comin' back tonight?" He jerked his head to indicate the direction of Tanner's truck and Luke found himself tensing.

"Not your business."

Luke immediately regretted his tone and the way he'd bristled. Gave too much away to a man who obviously missed nothing.

"Just took you longer to finish up than I thought."

"What the—" Luke found himself taking an aggressive step forward. "Were you spying on us?" He hadn't seen or heard anything. Hadn't sensed being watched. "Mind your own damn business."

"I was," he said, shrugged, and took another swallow of beer. "Colt Ewing. Don't think we got around to that earlier."

Luke blew out a breath. Was it only this afternoon? Felt like a week ago at least. "Luke Wilder." He took a deep swig of beer.

Thought about grabbing another but didn't want to turn his back on Colt.

Luke thought of something to say then disregarded it. "Can't begin to imagine what's going through your mind," he finally said.

The silence hummed between them, not uncomfortable, really, which was to Luke probably weirder than not feeling strange and awkward and even guilty even though he had done nothing wrong.

"You think it's true?" Luke finally asked, surprised the

guy wasn't peppering him with questions.

The shrug made the question irrelevant.

"Not why I'm here. Talon said she asked you to take a paternity test. You gonna make trouble?"

"What?"

The whole day just got weirder. First, Luke didn't make trouble. He'd grown up as the peacekeeper between his mother and the world. And second, he'd been accused of fathering a child with a woman he was pretty convinced he hadn't met to even have sex with. Damn. That would be one hell of an awkward super power, and the paternity test had been more of a demand.

"Trouble about what?"

Colt had thrown the first punch. Well, maybe that had been him, but he'd shoved him hard enough that his ribs still felt sore as hell, and he was beginning to think a couple might be cracked from his graceless fall to the floor, and that was before he planned to climb on a bull. He was glad he hadn't entered the saddleless bronc riding as well this time around.

"I don't give a shit about the results," he said. "I'm adopting Parker. We'll take care of him. Not asking you for anything."

*But some cheek cells.* Tanner had told him what it entailed.

"Then why the test?"

And the silence again. But it was peaceful. Luke realized

he'd never been with another person who didn't pulse and surge with a cackling, wild energy. His mother was a whirlwind, a diva, dramatic, fairly bursting out of her skin, and Kane was loud, fun, full of life, except before he mounted a bull then he went somewhere else entirely, and Luke had never been able to describe or explain it.

"Talon didn't have a family growing up," Colt finally said, his eyes narrowed, looking far away at something that wasn't there. "She's not going to walk away from the possibility of an extended family, and I won't try to cut you out of Parker's life, but if you're going to try to take him away from her if the results are positive then"—his physical gaze swung back into a micro-focus on Luke—"you and I will have trouble."

The cold, matter of fact way he said each deliberate word was definitely a threat, but Luke had been around the rodeo for a decade, and in a rodeo school before that. He didn't spook easily, and he couldn't fault the man for protecting a kid he wanted, and the woman he wanted. Then something occurred to him.

"Boy or girl?"

"Boy. Seven."

Luke thought about that. Seven years ago. No more like eight. He would have been maybe twenty. How he'd acted. Thought or, more accurately, hadn't thought, but he had always used condoms. Even pretty drunk he'd used condoms. Always.

"Talon tell you I wanted you to get the test, too?"

What might have passed as a ghost of a smile was gone before Luke could fully register it.

"Yeah. I left Marietta at eighteen. Didn't come back until April. Haven't been stateside much, but Talon isn't sure the cowboy Jenna felt she'd fallen in love with was from Marietta. All she knows is that they met at a rodeo and Jenna brought Talon back the next year and the year after that to try to find him. Jenna doesn't seem like the most reliable narrator so"—Colt broke off and took another swig of his beer—"I can't say I'm one hundred percent certain about Jenna."

Luke felt an unwelcome and unexpected prickle of shame. He couldn't exactly judge there.

"I'm with Talon now. It's different. My Life." For a moment Colt's voice softened fractionally with what sounded like awe and Luke now felt a stab of envy, which was stupid because he had nothing to complain about.

He was having one of his best years on the circuit. He was healthy and had recently landed his dream job with the IBR, so why was he getting all squishy with analysis?

"I'm going to be totally faithful to her in every way but, fuck, I've been thinking about it and I've been with a lot of women."

Luke choked. Bit back a totally inappropriate laugh, but it still burbled up, rent the calm between them, the night and the quiet, and he couldn't stop for a full thirty seconds.

"Damn my ribs still hurt from this afternoon," he said to break the tension. "You're built like a block of granite." He complained to Colt, but in a way, it was also a compliment.

"What's funny?" Colt's voice was so terse it could cut steel.

"What you said about being with women. I was just thinking the same thing before I found you on my door. I've never had a long-term relationship. Don't know how. Not proud of that." He couldn't help the glance across the grounds where a few trucks were already lined up with rodeo staff who were extras or more local so they didn't need a full trailer for the weekend. Already twelve other trailers had joined his. By tomorrow midmorning this area would be packed.

"My mom." He paused. Should he say our mom? Too soon probably. "She's real smart. Successful now. Land rights attorney but, growing up, we didn't have much. She was"—he blew out a breath and let the silence sit for a while—"it's like she was broken in some way."

It occurred to him that maybe the reason she'd always been so damaged was standing next to him. "I think she was real tortured by her past and could never quite get above or beyond it, but…" He couldn't say the rest.

That he doubted his mother had given up her baby by choice. That wouldn't help anything.

"She was eighteen when she had me. Sixteen when she had you." He pretended not to look, yet he did, but Colt didn't react. Not a flicker of expression. "It's like because of my dad, your dad too, she couldn't love again and, well, I always think of my brother, half brother really, to you and me, as the Romeo, total player, but I've had my share of fun."

Colt didn't respond and Luke wondered what was going through his head. He'd never been around a man harder to read and ranchers and cowboys were not known to wear their hearts or their thoughts on their sleeves. He braced for more questions about their mother or him or Kane. Hell, even the requested paternity test. He was jumping out of his skin about that though he was pretty certain it would be a big fat "no". Instead nothing, then Colt clinked his bottle with his.

"Something we had in common," he said.

Luke nodded. Were his casual weekend hookups going to be a thing of the past? It had been getting old now, but with his life, his schedule, how could it be different? He couldn't picture sticking with one woman in one town. What would it even be like? How would she handle him being gone so much? He drained the beer and then remembered the way Tanner's skin glowed in the truck, her smile, the way she hadn't pried but also hadn't ignored the situation, the way her hazel eyes sparkled when she laughed. He couldn't picture her as a weekend hookup. She wasn't that girl. She was a forever girl, and she might be giving out signs that she was fun and casual, but he didn't trust it.

"Talon's mine," Colt said, startling Luke out of his reverie. "She and Parker are the best thing that ever happened to me, and I'm not ever going to be stupid and do them wrong." His voice was quiet, matter of fact, but there was a ring of conviction in it that made Luke pause.

What would it be like to feel that finally he belonged with one woman? To not feel like a misfit, to be able to relax and be himself, come home to somebody. He remembered how Tanner had fixed his eye today, bullying him and teasing him even as she took care of him. Like he mattered.

"I've done enough wrong," Colt said into the silence, the night closing in further as the temperature dropped a little bit more. "But I will do Talon and Parker right."

Luke's heart thudded at the peace and determination he heard in Colt's voice. And again he couldn't stop his gaze from wandering to the left of his brother's powerful build to the outline of a familiar truck he could barely make out in the dark. Colt clapped him on the shoulder and walked off fluidly. Luke blinked, thinking that couldn't be it. They hadn't even begun to scratch the surface of what they needed to talk about, but when he took a surprised step intending to follow, Luke was alone in the field. He couldn't see any movement. Couldn't hear the rustle of clothing or thud of footsteps and Colt Ewing was a big man. But he was also stealthy as a spirit.

It spooked him how Colt seemed to vanish, like he'd been a figment of Luke's imagination only he would have imagined conversations with more explanations. More closure, but deep inside where he'd been so restless, so unsettled and if he were honest, more than a little angry, he felt at peace for the first time all day.

FOR ALL THE rodeos Luke had entered over the years, he had been to surprisingly few parades. Usually he was pulling into the rodeo grounds late Friday night, or early Saturday morning. The parades were for the community, the businesses, and the tourists. But wasn't the small-town folksy gathering exactly why he loved the rodeo over the more high tech, glossy marketing of the IBR Tour? He loved the kids lining Main Street with their smiling folks. The other kids, girl scouts, boy scouts, church groups, 4-H clubs, walking in the parade, dressed up in their uniforms, throwing candy, waving flags, holding glittery, homemade banners proclaiming their identity.

It just bled small-town closeness, families, love of the land and farming. A place to figure out who they were and who they wanted to be. Growing up in the one bedroom apartment in the grungy and graffitied urban sprawl of Phoenix, watching over Kane while their mom worked and went to school, Luke hadn't had time or money for any after-school activities or parades.

Watching the parade and later attending the rodeo meet and greets with the fans was probably as close as he was going to get to family. He had no idea how to be a dad. He hadn't had much more than a fly-by sperm donor, but he did think dads needed to be home, participate, lead by example, not be on the road visiting stock contractors and risking their lives for the thrill of competing. And that was why he picked up women who weren't like Tanner. Tanner oozed small-town cowgirl and ranch down to her bones. No way would she be a weekend hookup with a cowboy, which made her passionate kiss last night puzzling.

And his reaction, off the chart crazy. He'd had a hell of a time not giving into the fire she'd sparked. He'd lain awake half the night trying not to think how soft her skin was, how intriguing her freckles were, how her plump, defined lips felt so perfect against his. She was off limits to all but business transactions. Landing his first solo IBR account couldn't be complicated by emotions, and Tanner's fun, teasing personality combined with her brains and hint of vulnerability occasionally peeking through all of her steel would balloon to an unwieldy complication if he didn't keep his hands and other parts to himself.

So why had he'd said yes to her casual invitation to the parade? He was playing with fire, much like Kane did, only Kane had a tendency to go through life in a fireproof suit. Luke? Not so much. He had the scars to show that karma burned.

Tanner stood on tiptoe and brushed her lips against his ear, whispered something about the Marietta band, and almost reflexively his arm curved around her slim waist. He spread his fingers to feel more of her taut body and small swell of her hips. She was so slim, but strong. Not skinny, and a fantasy of her legs wrapped around his waist had him shifting positions, but not removing his hand.

She leaned into him a little and it felt right. *She* felt right and the dismay hit him hard.

"You're not wearing one of your rodeo buckles," she said, her fingers dancing along his belt, and he sucked in his breath.

She could make him hard with a teasing comment and nonsexual touch that he wished would become sexual. Imagine the havoc she could wreck if he gave into his impulse to take her hand and… he stopped that train of thought with an imaginary left hook. Family spot.

"Bit too show-off for me," Luke said.

"The Seventy-Eighth Copper Mountain Rodeo design is a real beauty," Tanner said. "Maybe one of the board members will let you see it."

"They'll be awarding it to me," Luke said because what else could he say?

Plus he loved the way her hazel eyes widened as her mouth slid into a sweet smile.

"We'll see, cowboy. You'll need to model it for me later," she said.

"Maybe, if you play your cards right, I'll even let you wear it." He teased back, easy in her company.

She nudged him with her body. “I’ll take you up on that because I love shiny and sparkle and I’ve always played a killer hand of poker.”

“Figures,” he said, forgetting his self-regulatory lectures from last night.

Tanner wasn’t a child. And if she wanted to play? Why the hell was he acting like spinster aunt? Tanner was a woman, not a girl. A businesswoman not a buckle bunny. Why not let loose a bit? Play with fire. Learn if her pale skin was as soft and warm as he imagined, and if she had freckles on more than her face. He really wanted to know that.

“Have I tortured you enough, cowboy, with small-town festivities?”

Her cheeks were flushed and her eyes shone, and he found himself smiling into her upturned face.

“Torture?” He bent down as if to kiss her lips and then thought maybe that was too presumptuous and public for a local girl, so he found her ear instead and graced the curved lines with his lips. “I think you’re enjoying the horses and their spangly riders and being pelted with candy as much as I am.”

She laughed and swung her body around to face him.

“I do love the parade and I used to be one of those spangled and sparkly riders with studded rhinestone chaps and a lot of fringe.”

“And the curls with a gallon of hairspray making them slap instead of bounce on your shoulders.”

"Nah, always a braid girl. My hair is a force of nature if I free it. Think tornado, class five."

"Now that I want to see."

And just like that her smile faded, her eyes were uncertain. "My sister has beautiful hair. It's a deeper red, more auburn than mine, and it's softer, less kinky, and she's wicked with the products and wields a mean blow dryer and curling iron so she can make it tumble over her shoulders like a field of poppies."

Her voice was flat, but he heard the echo of an ache in it. Sibling rivalry, or the expectation of it, he could totally relate to, especially coming up on the short end himself most of the time, despite being the older brother. He found himself holding her closer, resting his chin on top of her head, the straw of her cowboy hat, dark blue today, teased his chin.

"I've always been real partial to storms," he said. "The wilder the better, no pun intended."

"I think the pun was definitely intentional."

"Caught."

Her breathing quickened and the slight movement he glimpsed in the narrow "V" of her shirt was all it took to jack him up from teasing to serious. On a street corner of a town he'd sworn never to visit. With hundreds of people lined up watching Marietta smile and wave and toss candy as they marched proudly by on a warm September midmorning. With a woman five minutes ago he was counseling himself to keep his hands and other body parts to himself with.

Definite fail on that angle, and he was finding himself not really caring. Life was meant to be lived not watched on the sidelines like it was a damn parade and he was waiting for some small treat to be thrown his way.

His hands slid up to her waist, loving how small she felt, and he spanned his fingers so his thumbs brushed against the small swell of her breasts. Her heartbeat kicked up a notch.

"You don't have to sweet talk me, cowboy," she whispered and then whimpered when he kissed along her slender, pale neck.

"My timing sucks," he said as the high school band blared by them. He brushed his hardening erection against her, loving the flare of heat in her eyes. "Think of something mundane to distract me."

"Ummm…" Her green-flecked eyes drifted down to his mouth and stayed there.

"Not helping," he said softly.

Tanner's body seemed to melt into his. "Not really sure I want to help," she said softly, her fingers caught in the front of his shirt. "You mentioned candy last night. Red rope licorice, right?"

He nearly choked. "That was not to eat so still not helping." His mouth moved back and forth barely brushing across her lips.

"I wonder what it was for?" She said thoughtfully and tipped his Stetson back and caught it in one hand while her other feathered through his hair. "Do you really want help, cowboy?"

"Desperately." He let his hands span a little higher. "Considering we're on Main Street during the height of happy family time and my experiences yesterday all point to me being jailed or at least run out of town instead of just the best bar if I even think about what I'd like to do with you, cowgirl."

"I think I can get you reinstated"—she stood on tiptoe, her lips just a breath from his—"to Grey's if you behave."

"Trying." He anchored his hands on her hips.

"That's not what I meant by behaving." She sighed as she leaned into him. "But your way is probably for the best."

"Aaah-huh." He let go of her waist and intended to step away, but she made the mistake of looking up at him and the expression in her face, so warm and hungry booted his self-restraint. He cupped her cheeks. "I want to kiss you," he said. "I really blew it last night and couldn't sleep. I kept wondering how sweet you taste."

"Since most of the town is here, you'll need to settle for cotton candy." She snagged a bag from a passing vendor.

She dug in her pocket for a few dollars. She opened the bag and tore off a piece of spun sugar and held it out to him.

"Too pink?"

"I like pink."

"That's right. You're a metrosexual, twenty-teens man."

"No idea what that means," he said, closing his mouth around the treat.

He held her gaze as the sugar dissolved in his mouth and he pretended it was her mouth he was tasting. Bad idea, because he became harder, but he didn't care. Tanner made everything fun.

"But if sexual is involved then I'm listening." He tore off a bit of the cotton candy and held it out for her. "This pink isn't nearly as pretty as your lips or as sweet."

"How would you know, cowboy?" She asked, but color swept over her cheeks leaving him comparing the sweet to a different pink, which it again came out on the losing end of distraction tactics.

"I'd like to find out," he whispered a fraction from her lips, which pouted a little as if they were already attuned to his desire.

"Just to prove a point?" She challenged, her eyes alight with mischief and desire, and damn near impossible to resist.

"Just to kiss you."

The parade faded from his peripheral vision, the music and chatter and downhome sounding announcer faded.

"What. Are. You. Waiting. For?" Each word was a little puff of air that mingled with his and somehow that was more arousing than actually kissing her, imagining that their breaths intermingled.

"A smaller audience," he said ruefully, his forefinger traced town the line of her slender neck and settled in the hollow of her throat.

He wanted to kiss her there, along her collarbone. The

way her bones were so prominent looked vulnerable and elegant. He wanted to taste her skin. Drink in her scent.

"We could go back to the fairgrounds," she said.

He wanted to trace that line with his tongue.

"To…to…" She blinked. "Check my bulls." She finally managed.

"Is that what they call it these days?"

His conscience, which had been riding him so hard yesterday was apparently on strike today. He wouldn't let it go too far. Just a little fun. And she had mentioned bulls.

Yeah. Right.

THEY STROLLED BACK, arms around each other, not talking, but it felt so intimate, as if by being with Luke Wilder, she was sharing herself, and he was sharing back. The silence was peaceful yet hummed with expectation. What was she doing? Tanner demanded of her inner siren. She was supposed to be establishing a business relationship with Luke Wilder, not steamy sexual memories, which would most likely burn up her dreams for months to come. But her siren didn't care. Yesterday he had been more reserved. Today he seemed less tense, and she had to seize the day, so to speak. Not just think about what she wanted but go for it. Much like she'd implemented all the changes at the ranch rather than waiting for her daddy to give her permission and admire her work ethic and ideas.

Good Girl. Responsible Girl. Never-Complaining Girl. Hard-Working Girl. Why did that always have to be her? And had it really made her happy, blissfully happy?

Hell, no!

Luke's hand was around her waist and she savored the contact. He stopped, tangled his fingers in hers. They walked across the bridge and she dug two pennies out of her jeans.

"Make a wish?" She handed one to Luke.

He looked a bit surprised and then tossed it in the river.

"You better have made a wish." She chided. "And that looked like a lame effort."

"Show me."

She turned around so her back was against the wooden railing. Closed her eyes, rubbed the penny between her palms, made a wish, yes about him, and then tossed it over her left shoulder.

She opened her eyes and expected him to laugh at her or tease her about the childish ritual. Instead his golden eyes had darkened and the expression in them made it hard to breathe. He took her hand, looked at it a moment, and then linked fingers with her. They walked over the bridge and onto the grassy fair grounds.

"Bulls?" he asked.

"Jorge and a team are with them now," she said, feeling like she was practically issuing him an invitation to strip her and take her right here in the no longer open field because it was teaming with people, probably many of them acquaintances, and packed with trailers and motorhomes of rodeo competitors and support staff.

"In that case..." He looped the two long ropes of red licorice around her neck and let them dangle.

Tanner's heart galloped and her stomach dropped as the words hung, suspended in the air between them, drawn out, and she felt she was holding her breath.

"Yes," she said, nibbling on her lip nervously, not sure if she were making a statement or asking a question.

She'd never wanted a man so much. It was unnerving. The want. It was alive, clawing through her body, and it put her in a very vulnerable position. The want made her so unequal because no way could Luke Wilder, All-around cowboy who rode broncos and bulls like other men rode bikes, be that into her. Even her fantasies weren't that ambitious.

Luke unlocked the door to his Airstream trailer. He swung it open and Tanner walked in her insides burbling with excitement, desire, and nerves.

"Listen..." She grabbed his belt buckle. "I know women probably say this a lot to you, but I don't do this often," she said in a rush, trying to moisten suddenly dry lips.

"Cowgirl"—he put his hands on her hips—"I'm not interested in what other women do or don't do or say or don't say. It's just you and me here, and I don't have any expectations so don't worry and don't drag any pasts in here."

She swallowed hard. God, she was so bad at this, and he

was just so good. Kind in a way not a lot of men had been kind to her. It was ridiculous, really. He was so far out of her league he was a different sport, and she was going to blow it by chickening out and dumping all her insecurity in front of him. How had her friend Talon tossed aside every fear and jumped into bed with the Colt after a little more than twenty-four hours? Where could Tanner find some of that brashness?

"This is more like something my sister, my twin would do," she said staring at his shirtfront and tangling her fingers in the fabric between his western-style buttons.

He captured her fingers and brought them to his mouth. He kissed each one slowly until she raised her eyes to his. She felt warm and reassured. The caramel of his eyes made her feel like she was melting.

"Definitely not interested in your sister. It's just us, Tanner," he said, and she noticed he had kept the trailer door open. "Your sister's not here. And if she were, I'd tell her to get the hell out except more politely if you wanted me to."

She smiled. "I'm being stupid."

"No." He stepped in closer, pulled off her hat, and put it carefully on the counter by the small sink. "Just maybe jumping ahead of ourselves. There's no rush." He smiled, and her heart flipped over. "We can talk. Listen to music. I've seen some of your moves with a broom." He turned her and did a gentle quickstep around the small area of the trailer's living space.

He pulled her hips in to tightly align with his. She could feel his hard length, and the longing that swept through her stole her breath. She was being stupid. She really, really liked him. And IBR business or not, Luke Wilder was a nice guy. He was kind and fun and beautiful and he wouldn't have sex with her and then not look at her bulls objectively. She just knew it. He radiated respect and honesty in a way not a lot of people had in her life.

"Smooth moves, cowboy." She tugged him closer and found herself pressed up against the table. She plucked his hat off and put it on her head then stood on her tiptoes, spearing her fingers through his hair. "Widow's peaks are totally genetic." She mused, her eyes roving over his thick, springy hair and carved features. "Although it is a myth that it is controlled by one gene with two alleles, and I love how your hair grows back from your forehead," she said lightly, pretending to be less affected than she was.

She traced his widow's peak and resisted the urge to wrap herself around him, hook her leg around his waist, and align her body with all that hard, hot masculinity. "I bet all the buckle bunnies say that." She teased.

He made a face, and she mentally kicked herself.

"It doesn't matter what other women have and haven't said but, for the record, no one's even mentioned the whatever that word was about my hairline."

*Insecure much?*

It wasn't as if she hadn't been with a few guys in college

and grad school. Just no one as innately masculine as Luke. And, to be honest, which she brutally was with herself all the time, no one she'd been this madly attracted to. And for so long. She'd done a summer college internship at a huge ranching operation well outside of Denver and part of her job had been traveling the Mountain circuit, and she'd first seen Luke hop off a bull after the buzzer, briefly grin at the crowd, and not even look at his score before he swung himself over the fence back into the staging area. He'd known he'd killed. He'd known he'd jumped far out into first place. He'd gotten the job done and he walked by her with his smooth walk and a head nod that had made her weak-kneed. She'd seen him ride in other rodeos and each time he was a thing of beauty, and she'd been back stage after each ride, eating him up with her eyes, and yet he hadn't remembered seeing her, even being briefly introduced to her during a meet and greet with the stock contractors.

Well, she smiled up into those melting golden eyes. She was going to make sure he remembered her this time.

"So, cowboy…" She let her thumb trace his bottom lip and he sucked it into his mouth.

Desire shot straight through her. With her other hand, she tucked her finger between the snaps on his Western shirt and popped one open, let her finger brush against his warm chest before she slid lower and popped another snap open.

He was beautiful. Honey golden, smooth chest, and lightly ripped. Nothing too bulgy like he sweated it out at a gym, but not an ounce of extra fat that she could see. And she was looking. She placed her palm on his tight, toned abs, wondered if she had the nerve to use the licorice, and decided maybe she should wait a bit on that. "You got any more moves you want to show me, cowboy?"

Her voice had gone husky and her hand trembled.

He covered her hand with his, and leaned forward, his golden eyes burning. A sound escaped from the back of her throat like he was unlocking her soul, she thought more than a little dramatically.

He kicked the trailer door shut. Flipped the lock.

"Tanner." He cupped her jaw with one palm and his fingers tugged at her braid to pull her head back a bit. "I'll show you anything you want."

*Best answer ever.*

And that was the last gasp of her brain synapses as Luke's lips parted hers, his tongue sliding in to tease the seam of her mouth. His hands trailed fire down her body and she tugged his shirt aside so she could run her palms over his chest, and his shoulders, and his back, and she still didn't get enough. She eased the fabric away from his shoulders kissing him, loving the flex of his defined muscles.

The heat from his skin. She pressed a line of kisses across his hammering heart before tonging his nipple. He groaned her name and pulled her hair out of its elastic and ran his fingers through her hair.

*This is happening. It's really happening.*

She would have pinched herself, but her hands were too busy touching his hot skin. Michelangelo couldn't have created a better torso on his best day with his David.

"It's like a cloud of fire." He breathed against her mouth, pressing against her further back so her butt hit the hard edge of the table. He lifted her up onto it and stepped between her legs.

"Yes." She hissed, pulling off his shirt all the way and tossing it over his shoulder even as she assertively grabbed the buckle on his belt to get to the zip on his jeans.

"Thanks, but I already got a shirt."

Luke swore and spun around blocking her from whoever had come into the trailer.

"What the hell are you doing here?"

"Nice to see you too big brother." He emphasized the word big and laughed.

Tanner quickly checked her clothes. Mostly together, but her heart was pounding and not in a good way and her cheeks were nine or ten shades of red probably.

"Ever hear of knocking? Give me my shirt."

"I did knock. Twice. And called out and since I'd seen you both come in here, I thought I'd better make sure you were okay. Not needing oxygen or anything."

"I locked the door."

Shit-eatin' grin. He dangled a key. "Used to be mine. You wanted me to keep a key in case."

"Shirt."

"Don't know, brother. Your girl gave it to me."

Tanner winced and waited for Luke to deny the "your girl" comment.

"Shirt."

Tanner poked her head around Luke's spectacular chest, which was unfortunately disappearing back under his shirt. Tanner sucked in her breath, when six-foot-plus pushed himself off the trailer door and held his hand out for her to shake like this was a social situation. His eyes were like Mercury and definitely brimming with amusement.

She'd seen him in a lot of IBR ads and in commercials, but none of those began to do him justice and being in such a closed space with two spectacularly, masculinely beautiful specimens hurt her eyes and brain and was devastating to her ego. Tucker would have been thinking twosome. Tanner was thinking escape.

"Kane Wilder." He continued to hold out a large, calloused hand, and Tanner shook it automatically, trying to shake off her embarrassment and shock and disappointment, all of which warred for supremacy.

They were grown adults. She shouldn't feel like a teen caught out by her dad, but she did.

"The prettier brother, I heard," she mumbled.

Kane smiled wider. "Now that's just Luke bein' mean,"

"What are you doing here, Kane?"

"Tryin' to keep mom from simultaneously having a heart attack, stroke, and aneurysm while burning down the town and dragging your sorry, naked butt behind that new hot little red Audi convertible she just bought because you haven't been taking her calls. And now I know why."

Luke flipped his brother off. "Can we do this happy reunion later? Like never," he muttered.

"No worries." Tanner slid off the table. "I gotta get back to work."

"So that's what you call takin' a break," Kane drawled. "Now I know why you like the rodeo circuit, big brother. Much friendlier."

"Shut the fuck up, Kane," Luke said, more tersely than she'd heard him speak before.

He turned back toward her, his hands covering her ears as if he could help her to unhear Kane's teasing. "Sorry," he said softly, his lips brushing hers, and her toes curled at the sensation and warmth in his voice and gaze. He still hadn't buttoned his shirt and her eyes ping-ponged between his heated, honey gaze and beautiful, tanned, sculpted chest that begged to be touched.

"I'll see you later." Luke spoke low in her ear, his body never breaking contact.

She tried to stop the rush of pleasure, of happiness that he still wanted to see her and that he wasn't playing it cool in front of his brother, and utterly failed. She felt giddy, and her body still hummed as if it hadn't gotten the email that the physical touch was over for now.

"Sure," she said, suddenly shy with Kane watching them,

his dark hair was longish, past his jaw line and his eyes were a disarming, light blue, almost silver-grey, and she felt like he could see all the way through her. He looked friendly and amused, but there was a coiled tension in him that belied the charm. Tanner was too much around animals not to be able to read the dominant ones that could get dangerous quickly.

"Later," she said as breezily as she could as if she got caught stripping men she'd technically known less than twenty-four hours all the time.

*No. That would be Tucker.*

Tanner managed to somehow unglue herself from Luke, who swung open the door and walked down the two stairs to the grass. She had the impulse to kiss him again, but there were too many people around, many whom she'd known growing up, plus she could see his brother, definitely hot and gorgeous and laughing at the situation, lounging against the same table she'd been aiming to use as the launch pad to vanquish her sexual drought.

Luke seemed to read her mood because he leaned forward to kiss her then hesitated. Instead his hands gently framed her face and then touched her hair so reverently.

"Your hair is beautiful," he said. "It glows."

She batted his hand away. She'd forgotten it was down. It was elevated around her face like an embarrassed and very off course halo.

"I love it," he said, giving her the elastic back that he'd put around his wrist. "Wear it down Saturday night."

"Are you nuts?" She demanded.

"Please."

That undid her.

"You free later? For the barbeque this afternoon or tonight? I saw a flyer in that Big Z's Hardware store yesterday about it."

She hesitated a second.

"Please."

"But your brother."

"Can find his own date."

"Your mother?"

"She can definitely find her own date."

Tanner laughed, knowing he was trying to make light of an awkward situation. She did feel a little lighter inside and walked away backwards, finding it hard to say goodbye. She kissed her fingers and waved to him before spinning around and walking away fast, willing him to look away. To not notice her limp, not worry about her, not speculate on her limitations and to not treat her differently.

LUKE JOGGED BACK up the steps.

Kane leaned against the table, grin wide. "All the shit you've flipped me about my behavior over the years."

"Why are you really here?" Luke demanded, arms crossed, not that surprised Kane had shown up, since Luke had been dodging his mom's increasingly short and irritated phone calls, but he still would have appreciated some warning. Make that a lot of warning.

"Red, huh?" Kane ignored the question and picked up Tanner's hat from the counter and spun it around on his finger. "Little slow off the mark, brother. All you got off was her hat, and she had you half undressed and was reaching for the goods. I definitely could have timed it better. Given the girl another minute. Could have gotten an awful pretty picture." He held up his cell phone. "Maybe could have started my retirement account with a few naked shots of you."

Luke didn't take the bait.

"Damn, you still have no sense of humor. Not like you haven't walked in on me."

"Your door was open," Luke said coolly, mentally trying to unsee the image of his then sixteen-year-old naked brother in full sexual-conqueror mode with a college girl several years older. He closed his eyes and pinched the bridge of his nose.

"True." Again Kane grinned. "Thought you said you were done with red. Couldn't resist working your way through the family tree?"

"What's that supposed to mean?"

Kane laughed. "Right, Romeo."

He looked at Luke, his grey gaze questioning. "You don't know?" he finally asked. "Damn, Luke. You really need to ask more questions."

# Chapter Eight

"ABOUT?"

"Like what the T stands for."

"Cut the cryptic crap."

"Tucker T."

Luke rolled his eyes. That was almost five years, and yeah he'd been hurt and embarrassed and so stupid at the time. Definitely not a shining moment, but Kane usually stuck to more current barbs. Kane lived to taunt him, like he knew more than everybody else. Probably did, too. It had killed their mother when Kane hadn't gone to college. He could have. Kane's father, who'd done everything he could to forget Kane existed had been thrilled to fund his education when he'd seen Kane's academic load and GPA. Kane was ridiculously smart but, instead, he'd graduated early and headed out to a rodeo school in California run by a former three-time, bull-riding champion who taught yoga, meditation, Zen and other touchy feeling shit Luke had never had time for.

But the name Tucker T was a low punch in the gut even

for Kane.

"Way in the past, Kane," he said flatly.

"You never asked her why Tucker T?"

"Some alliterative performing name. Fake like everything else," he said, trying to shrug it off, but instead a deep dread took hold as he saw Kane counting off seconds on his fingers like he'd always done when Luke had been slower on the uptake about everything than he had been.

*No. Fucking. Way.*

"Tucker McTavish. Triple T Ranch. Montana born and bred. One half of the McT twins, barrel racers and rodeo darlings in their early teens.

Luke stared, speechless at his brother, forgetting even to breathe.

"Twin sister to Tanner McTavish. Geneticist and former star barrel racer. Took a crippling fall at fifteen. Four months in a Seattle hospital far from home and family and never competed again. Ring a bell."

*Oh, hell no. No. No. No. Impossible even with his shitty luck this weekend in this town.*

Kane, who always did his research, and could quote the stats of every bull rider on the US Tour as well as Australia, Mexico, and Canada like he was some kind of savant, laughed at Luke's obvious horror and became a mind reader as well.

"Ah, hell yes," he said.

Luke's mind went blank. His body turned to stone. He

couldn't even dredge up the fiercest, most heartfelt curse of all.

He leaned back and let his head hit the cupboards above his stove once, twice, three times. What karmatic god had he pissed off to deserve this weekend? It hadn't even officially hit the weekend, or the rodeo and he couldn't tangle with gravity to bottom out any lower.

"Hey, now, you may need a few of those brain cells left to apologize."

How the hell could he apologize for that? He'd slept with Tanner's twin over the course of a few rodeos, and there hadn't been much sleeping involved. He hit his head again, eyes closed as if he could shut out the image of Tucker, all curves, siren smile, auburn hair curling down her back, sparkling, emerald eyes promising heaven, reeling him in like a prize marlin over and over. Until she cut him loose to snag another cowboy after a few weeks of Luke following her around dazed and thinking himself in love. And then she'd cut that poor bastard loose for another. She'd laughed at Luke and shrugged off his attempt to discuss their relationship.

He could still hear her musical voice low with a husky note, see the astonishment in her eyes, the disdain on her beautiful, bow shaped candy red lips. "What relationship? It was sex Luke. Just sex. Better than most I must admit, but still just sex. Grow up. Men do it all the time. Thought you were a big boy but you're acting like a big baby whose toy was taken away. I'm not your toy. I'm not yours. I'm my own person."

Still burned him how he'd read her so wrong. He'd been totally infatuated. He hadn't listened to anyone when they'd tried to warn him, but he was new to the California circuit. And he'd left mid-season because he couldn't stand watching her hook up with different men each weekend. He'd felt like such a stupid idiot. He'd just turned twenty-three and thought he definitely should have known better.

He'd joined the Mountain Rodeo Circuit and found a job at a bull-breeding ranch in Colorado and tried to put the whole moment of madness behind him. He'd been caught up in the fairy tale that his mom used to tell him about. How, when she'd seen his dad, it had been magic. She'd known he was her soul mate, her true and only love. It had seemed like love the first time he'd seen Tucker T take a practice run, jump off her horse, and shoot him the most smokin' hot, sexual appraisal he'd ever been exposed to and ten minutes later he'd been in his trailer thinking about making himself a sandwich when she'd shown up with a bottle of champagne and wearing ripped jeans that barely qualified as clothing and leather lingerie. He hadn't been into the champagne but he'd definitely appreciated the other.

Love. How stupid he'd been. He'd been as blind as his mother. Luke banged his head back again.

"Climb off your guilt horse," Kane said. "From what mom said, you're banged up enough from the bar fight, which I'm totally pissed I missed. Besides, you didn't even know Tanner then." Kane shrugged it off. "You thinking of signing her to a stock contract for the tour? Which tier? Anything I might be interested in? She got some bulls at Copper Mountain Rodeo we can check out?" Kane had gone from teasing to professional in a blink.

Bulls? How could his brother think about bulls at a time like this, the self-absorbed prick? Every shy look of uncertainty he'd seen chase across Tanner's face when the topic of her twin came up lanced through him like a hot poker. No wonder she thought a man wouldn't be sexually interested in her, growing up with that breath-stealing, beautiful, calculated sex-on-a-stick man collector.

He groaned and banged his head again.

He had to tell Tanner. Had to before he took it any further, not that there'd be a further after the revelation, which would be for the best, so why did disappointment settle over him like an early snow? Luke hadn't been involved in the stock business long, but he knew a deal-breaker when he saw one.

Kane slapped his back. "Get over the mea culpa. This isn't your usual circuit and Tucker's in California so, yee haw, ride 'em, cowboy. No need to go all confessional prematurely so avoid the hassle and just have a good time. Not like you're setting up your rig in Marietta permanently. Now let's go check out the stock." Kane rubbed his hands together in anticipation and Luke swallowed the urge to puke.

The fact he was bothered he was going to lose a chance with Tanner sucked, but what was worse was how much it burned. He tried to tell himself that feeling something for her was bad news, and he should be relieved to shut any of that shit down, but he wasn't listening to his so-called wiser self, which should not have been sleeping earlier when he'd invited her back to his trailer.

He liked Tanner. He was attracted to her, but it wasn't just sexual. It was… hell. He had to stop thinking this way. He had to get on the back of a bull in twenty-four hours, and he could not have his mind on Tanner or his dumb ass, naïve infatuation with her sister five years ago. Or his maybe brother. Or his mom. Or anything else but the ride.

"What the hell is wrong with you?" Kane demanded. He was already down one step on the trailer and still eye level with Luke. "You still strung up with Tucker?"

"Hell, no." Luke had no hesitation on that front. None.

No he was strung up, in the words of his brother, on Tanner. He'd been a punk with Tucker. He was a man now, and he could tell the difference between lust and feelings, and he didn't think Tanner was going to be an easy chord to cut. But cut it he must, because long-term relationships were out, and a relationship with a woman who lived and breathed Marietta had mega-disaster stamped all over it.

TANNER WAS MEASURING out feed when Jorge drove up with her father. It took him several minutes to get out of the truck. Tanner pretended not to notice and Jorge pretended he had an email on his phone to read while Bruce McTavish coordinated his four limbs and pushed himself out of the truck. He left his cane in the cab. Tanner's lips tightened.

Her dad tried to pretend the accident hadn't happened. He tried to pretend he hadn't had compression fractures in his chest, broken legs as well a closed head injury that had left him in a coma for almost a month.

"Feels good to be back," he said, each word deliberately spoken thanks to over a year of speech therapy that had left the ranch in debt and struggling.

But the Triple T was back. All her fierce dedication and pushing of her father to complete his therapy both physical, speech, and language processing had paid off. She looked up.

"Yes," she said. "It is, Dad."

"You heard from your sister?"

"Tucker?"

"You got another?"

She resisted the urge to say "thank God, no." Her dad adored Tucker. She'd always been his favorite. Always. She looked like their mother, who, even though she'd left their family when she and her sister hadn't yet turned twelve, still held a piece of Bruce McTavish's heart.

"I wanted her to come home this weekend," He said after a long silence.

Tanner nearly dropped the bag of enriched blend of oats and grain. That was all she needed—Tucker. Tanner loved her sister. She admired her confidence. Her drive. Her focus to go after everything she wanted and then some. She admired her career, her sense of fun and daring, but next to Tucker she just… Tanner cut off the unproductive, but true, thought. She'd never had a date in high school because boys had only wanted Tucker. The friendships she would develop she'd soon learned were all about getting closer to Tucker. And when they'd been competing in teen barrel racing events, she'd won most of the events, but Tucker had received all the attention.

She hadn't been trying to be mean. She was just crazy charismatic, and she'd shrug off the latest boy or man defection and tell Tanner. "He's no prize if he tosses you at the first barrel. I'm saving you time and heartache."

It hadn't felt like that at the time. And it sure as heck wouldn't now to watch Luke turn away all dazzled by her beautiful twin so much so he'd probably not even remember Tanner's name or that he'd once kissed her dizzy.

Ugh. Enough with the pity party.

"Why do you want Tucker, Dad. She's got a commercial shoot and several sponsor events this weekend.

"You girls should be together," he said. "Talk."

He wouldn't look her in the eye. Tanner climbed down off of Hell's Bell's pen fence and walked toward her father.

"About what?" she asked.

Her father never wanted to talk so alarms were ringing everywhere.

Her father shuffled to another pen, using the fence. Her heart pinched and she had to force her hands to her sides so she wouldn't offer to help.

"Thinking she might settle by now. Ranch. Babies."

"Tucker?" Tanner laughed.

Her sister repeatedly said she never wanted to marry or have kids and she sure wasn't going to "be tied to one ranch and one town." She'd said that when she was twelve and she still said it at twenty-seven. And as far as the "M" word, Tucker would toss her flowing mane of amber fire over her shoulder and ask "Why? What's in it for me?" She always laughed and said there were "So many men and only one of me."

Tanner had always been a bit stunned by her sister's attitude and thought she must have taken after their mother rather than their dad. Tanner had always thought being married and having a family and working with animals on the ranch and growing a lot of her own food was the best way to live life. She'd enjoyed the intellectual challenge of college and grad school but she'd missed the ranch and her animals. She'd missed Marietta.

"When you going back to school?"

Tanner was so astonished by the question she nearly clapped her hand over her ear several times thinking she'd heard incorrectly.

"I'm done with school. I got my masters."

*Plus another year and a half.*

"You quit to come home and run the ranch when I couldn't."

She walked closer to her father and looked quickly around. For such a usually bustling place, the stock pens were strangely deserted as if her father had told their crew he needed a moment. Her stomach churned sickly. The few times her father had done a heart-to-heart, the outcome had never been good.

"What's this about?"

"You should finish what you start."

Her heart thumped unevenly. "What exactly are you referring to?"

"Get your doctorate so you can get that job you wanted in a lab or teaching at some fancy school." He spoke stiffly as if the words were alien in his mouth so he'd had to rehearse them over and over.

Tanner felt as if all the blood had rushed from her head.

"Dad?"

He walked to another pen and stood looking, swaying a little, looking at the bull, Rock 'N Roll inside.

"What's this about? I have a job. I work on our ranch. With you."

"Don't want you stuck on the ranch."

"I'm not stuck. I love it. I love the bulls and the horses. I love the ranch." Her voice rang out, getting a little high and strangled.

What was he saying? What could he possibly be saying? She knew the ranch had struggled. That they'd had to take out two loans, but she'd worked hard, cut back on staff, sold some good breeding stock and had worked really hard on their breeding program and marketing. They were climbing out of debt, not sliding back. She was only in phase one of her plan for the ranch.

He looked at her for a long moment, and Tanner felt as if she were looking at a stranger.

"You loved school."

"Yes. But I didn't study animal science and genetics to sit in some university lab."

"I'm beginning to think Tucker won't come home."

Tanner waved her hand as if she could wave away her absent sister.

"So what? She's living her life. She can come home anytime. The ranch will always be there for her."

Tanner spoke with finality, too uncomfortable with this conversation. Her dad was a man of action. Not words. And never feelings and this one-eighty scared her.

"It's no life to be alone on a ranch. No husband. No family."

Tanner could barely breathe. What wasn't he telling her? She opened her mouth to ask, but felt swamped by fear and confusion by his closed off expression.

"It's my life, Dad," she whispered. "What I want."

*Is he sick? What's he not saying?* She was felt like she was climbing out of her skin with anxiety.

"Your mom didn't want it."

*Or them.*

Tanner winced as the thought hit her. She still remembered the day she and Tucker had gotten off the school bus and run up the mile-long drive to find their dad feeding the animals like usual, but no mom. No snack. No dinner roasting in the oven.

"You're mom's gone," he'd said when Tucker had asked. "Don't know if she'll be back so you girls will need to take over the entire garden, cooking as well as other chores."

"I'm not mom, Dad."

Why was he talking like this? He never revisited the past. Ever.

"What's wrong?"

"Got an offer."

"What?"

"Thinking about it."

She couldn't move. Couldn't breathe. *An offer. Sell the ranch. The Triple T.* It had been her grandfather's and his father's before that. It was her home. Her business. Her history. These were her bulls. And her broncos, but she loved the bulls the most. Their fire. Their unpredictability. The beauty when they whirled around the arena, the rider. Her thoughts spun.

"Why… why would you ever sell the ranch?" She hated

that her voice broke, that she could barely get the words out. It wasn't just his ranch. It was hers. Hers and Tucker's. Their legacy. And when she had children it would be theirs.

"Just thinking."

*Well don't.*

She swallowed and so many words flowed around them, questions, fears, but she couldn't seem to grab any of them. She remembered how, when she was little, she and Tucker used to try to catch fireflies, running around, their fingers outstretched always reaching, never catching.

"Don't get a lot of offers on ranch property."

"But why would you even consider it?" She demanded.

"My ranch."

Tanner took a step back. He looked at her then looked away as if he saw too much.

His ranch. His. Not theirs. Not hers. It had been her home. Her business. Her future. But now he was saying not her anything.

His.

"Just thinking," he said gruffly after time stretched thin. "Got an offer. Thinking on it. That's all. You'd be free to live your own life."

"This is my life."

Tanner bit down on her lip, feeling like the dirt under her feet was sliding sideways and away. She needed to… she didn't know what to do. Argue? No arguing with Bruce McTavish. Go somewhere and process? But where? And how could she process this? The ranch. The bulls. The broncos. The breeding. The training and some boarding. This was her life. Blindly, she climbed up on a pen and looked over at her only all white bull, Rising Star.

"Hey, beautiful." She crooned, unable to see him through her tears, barely able to get the words out past the lump in her throat.

He chewed calmly and eyed her. Like nothing was wrong. And maybe it wasn't. She just needed to keep calm. Her dad was tired. Worried. He just needed to see she could take care of the ranch and the animals and the future. That was her family. The bulls. The horses. Her crew. Her dad was just feeling… who knew what he was feeling and who cared? He was wrong. And she'd prove it to him.

Tanner began to sing a Sara Bareilles ballad, like her father's bombshell hadn't exploded. Rising Star moved closer and she scratched his ears, and he tilted his head, momentarily abandoning his special grain protein mixture. She felt cheered as he snuffled at her. She fought the urge to hug him. That could go badly in a second, but she felt like she needed something warm and safe to hold on to.

"Don't let that IBR cowboy see you," her dad said, leaning against the pen fence and Tanner had to blink back tears because it was like the old times when she used to follow her dad around the rodeo, taking care of the bull and the bronco stock in between her qualifying rounds.

"That IBR know-it-all will think we're raising cows, not

bulls."

"The IBR know-it-all will think what?" Kane swung himself up on top of the pen fence next to her, the picture of masculine perfection. "Nice to see you again." He smiled cheekily and he had a cleft dimple in his chin. Of course he did.

"I bet."

"You wound me."

"Just a flesh wound," she said quickly and swung her leg around on the top of the pen so she could jump back down and get away from Mr. Charming and her father, who was gazing at Kane with awe. She jumped, bracing for the smack of the packed dirt, but instead hit warm, hard flesh.

"Hello," she said breathlessly, her lips inches from Luke's and, that fast, her dad, his bombshell, the stock pens, the bull-riding brother with lousy timing all disappeared.

His arms were hard around her body and she felt safe. It was heaven and spooked her to her soul. She relied on no one but herself. She had since she'd been fifteen and alone in the hospital, trying to heal from an injury she could barely comprehend that had changed her life beyond recognition.

She couldn't help it; her fingers crept from his shoulders, which she'd instinctively grabbed when he caught her, to touch his hair, which was so thick and soft. Her gaze settled on his mouth. He'd kissed her earlier. She wanted him to kiss her again, Kane and her father be damned.

"Cowboy," she said.

His eyes were liquid gold, and she knew he was going to kiss her. Her body heated and melted and her lips parted, but then his expression closed off and he put her down. Looked away. What the hell just happened?

# Chapter Nine

"WELL?" TANNER DEMANDED later that afternoon, her attention completely focused on Luke.

He took a bite into the dark chocolate, salted caramel, and lavender square and let it work its magic in his mouth. He wasn't that much of a candy or chocolate fan, but he was enjoying to Tanner's undivided focus a little too much.

"Good," he finally said, when he could talk.

"Good? That's the best you got?" She scoffed. "Sage Carrigan's chocolates are the best! She's a local and one of the first business owners to really wake up Marietta to the possibility of being a tourist destination. Her chocolates are destination chocolates, and I bet they could beat chocolates in France, Switzerland, and any other European country famous for chocolate. They are the best."

He found himself smiling inside. She held out the rest of the chocolate he'd taken a nibble from, silently daring him to finish it so he could praise it properly. He loved the way her skin gleamed and her pale freckles played across her skin like a star map. Her greenish, hazel eyes were free of the earlier shadows he'd seen when he and his brother had joined her to look at the stock she'd brought to supply the rodeo. He'd suggested they attend the town's barbeque and street fair after he and Kane had looked at the ten Triple T bulls, and they had watched as four more had been delivered.

Kane had inspired awe among everyone there. Luke didn't begrudge him the attention. He would have hated it. He loved riding. But it was a job. And he didn't want the other aspects of it. The social. The adoration. The demands of management and sponsors. The scrutiny. All he wanted he thought as he watched Kane turn it on was to get away with Tanner.

He leaned forward. "This chocolate can't begin to compare with how sweet you taste," he said softly, and then took the rest of it from her hand with his teeth and then leaned in close enough for her to take a bite.

He should tell her he knew Tucker. Had known her a long time ago. He'd been trying to carve out a time to tell her, make it casual, not a big deal, but he had a sinking feeling it would matter a lot to her so he wasn't thrilled to open the topic. He needed to, but between Tanner bumping into many friends—she seemed to know the entire town and Kane improbably tagging along, he hadn't had the chance.

And the more time they spent together, the more he wanted to put it off, but then it would get awkward to tell her later. And he really wanted there to be a later, which he was trying to not examine too closely, but "hey, Tanner, I think you're great and would love to try to see you again after this weekend, by the way I slept with your twin a few times, but that was over years ago," didn't exactly fit in with natural conversation.

Yet Tanner was so easy to talk to, so easy to be with. She was smart. Funny. Subtly sexy in an understated way that made him want to get closer, get to know her better. He loved her natural look. Her love for her bulls and their bloodlines. Her enthusiasm for life.

Tell her, he ordered himself, trying to signal Kane to get lost. Later was the coward's way, but the afternoon walk around Main Street and the park with the food booths, children's games, open shops and sidewalk sale was part of small-town life he loved but didn't get to often participate in. He wondered if Colt were here with Talon and her kid. Kane was going to give him hell about that when he found out. And he would find out. God, this rodeo. Heaven and hell so far.

He was competing tomorrow. He needed a clear head. No drama. Maybe he should tell her Sunday, after the finals. Not the best timing. Definitely not the honorable path. He squirmed internally because he always walked the right path, not the easy path. But two days wouldn't make that much of a difference, as long as he didn't sleep with her.

"You like caramel," he said as she closed her eyes and hummed as she took the first bite of the brownie, Rachel, owner of the Copper Mountain Dessert Company was selling from a festive, rodeo-themed table outside of her bakery.

He barely resisted kissing the corners of her mouth where she still had a crumb. She opened her eyes, her expression still blissful as she held out the brownie to him.

"I like caramel even better now."

"Why now?" he asked taking a bite.

She stood on tiptoe, kissed him, snagging a bit of the brownie for herself. Her lips brushed his, and without thinking, his hand pressed against the small of her back, keeping her close.

"Your eyes are caramel-colored," she said softly, pink staining her cheeks, but her gaze held his. "Only prettier."

Luke felt a jolt deep inside. He'd thought as long as he didn't let things get sexual before he told her about Tucker, he'd be okay. Maybe. At least not a jerk, but she was not making the not sexual plan easy to keep to.

He saw Kane had been waylaid by a group of young boys, all posturing a bit, trying to seem taller, bigger, older than they were while talking to his brother. Kane looked relaxed, interested. Luke liked meeting the younger fans, but Kane was just so much better at the social part. Luke felt tense, waiting for his mother to show up, but so far after her flurry of texts and phone calls yesterday, she'd been silent. Nor had she answered his early morning phone call to her.

"How hungry are you, Tanner?" he asked, part of him enjoying the small-town scene, the other dreading gossip, seeing his grandfather, the bartender, and Colt, so he was wishing them far away, but public would be better for keeping his promise of hands to himself.

"Very." She placed her palm flat against his abs. "We did come for the barbeque, and you're going to need your stamina for later."

"My stamina's fine," he said quickly, hoping she was referring his bull-riding and roping events and not anything else.

Just thinking about the possibility of anything else had his cock stirring with sudden interest, and his jeans felt restrictive, and not for the first time did he wish he was not so sexually suggestive. It would be better to play it cool, professional instead of adjusting his jeans and mentally dwelling on cold showers.

Tanner poured more fire on his desire by letting her gaze drift down his body real slowly so her once-over was as hot and suggestive as a caress. "You're right," she said. "I'm not talking about the stamina necessary for your hoped for eight second ride tomorrow."

Her eyes sparkled and she tangled her fingers with his and tugged him away from the bakery.

"That was not funny." He reeled her back in and nipped her earlobe.

"Yeah, it was." She laughed over her shoulder, and he had to hold back a smile.

"Not laughing," he said. "And I'm happy to compare

stamina any day, any time."

"I might take you up on that, cowboy," she said. "So let's get some real food in you."

TANNER LOVED THE rodeo. It was her favorite time of year. The weather was still usually sunny and warm during the day, but the nights held a whisper of fall. Her town was all dressed up, showing its best side, and she loved how most of the businesses had tables outside the their shops, showcasing their rodeo-inspired specialties. The town was alive with locals and tourists. The rodeo was a fun opportunity to show off her beautiful bulls and the Triple T Ranch and to catch up with friends. She tried to push her worries about her father's plans for the ranch and his revelation about an unexpected sales offer out of her mind at least for the weekend. Plenty of time to ask questions later. Grieve if necessary.

But maybe she needed to pin her dad down now. She could hardly offer up bulls she might no longer have. She felt sick, but the brush of Luke's fingers along her spine centered her. Her dad wouldn't sell. He was just feeling his age, his injury. She'd convince him. Or, worse, demand Tucker come home and work her magic. When Luke was long gone.

She kicked herself for her cowardice and insecurity, but at least it was a plan instead of just feeling anxious about the future. She might be living on borrowed time so she needed to make the most of it. Taking a deep breath, as if that would help her cleanse out the worries, Tanner looked around at her beloved Main Street.

She was surprised she hadn't run into Talon but maybe Colt was still processing the stunning news he had a brother and a half brother and a birth mother who wanted to connect with him. She wondered what she would feel if she learned her mother wanted to see her again. It had been so long, more than half her life. After her accident, she had wanted her mother to come visit her, take care of her, had cried for her, had begged her dad to try to find her, convinced her mother would come, but nothing. And it had been then she'd known deep down inside that her mother was gone, really gone, and no longer wanted to be a mother.

She still had no idea what she and Tucker had done wrong. How that abrupt departure was even possible. She couldn't imagine ever leaving a husband and two daughters, especially without a clue as to why or without a goodbye.

"That corn is going totally to waste." Luke poached the corn from her plate.

She grabbed for it, but he held it out of reach and laughed.

"That's better."

"How's being a thief better?" She demanded.

"You're smiling," he said, holding out the corn so she could take a buttery bite.

She sighed as the flavors melted in her mouth.

"You looked so serious before. Sad."

"Oh. Sorry."

"Don't apologize. What were you thinking about?"

He sounded like he was interested and it didn't occur to her to obfuscate. She wanted a real man so she too had to keep it real.

"Colt. Wondering how he was processing all this. You. And how I would feel if my mom suddenly came back." She was surprised how hard it was to get the words out. It became that much harder when he touched a few wispy curls that danced around her pale face after escaping from her braid. "She left when I was eleven."

*And now her dad was thinking of selling the ranch. Her home. Her business. Without consulting her.*

"Her loss," he said softly. "My mom was—" He broke off, frowned, and then put his plate off to the side on the wooden bench where they sat in Founder's Park. "She was a force of nature. Demanding. Volatile. Brilliant. Funny. So damn smart. She worked hard and went to school for a lot of my childhood, but she always stuck by us, never once wavered even when my dad left her for the second time."

He sat quietly, his eyes thoughtful, face pensive as he watched local kids run across the grass, chasing bubbles, chasing each other, being chased by parents who wanted them to eat one last bite or whatever, beef, corn, potato salad, green beans, baked beans, berries. Tanner wondered what he was thinking, feeling. Was this a side of family life he didn't see very often?

"I can't imagine walking away and never looking back." He admitted, his expression looking so haunted that Tanner felt herself ache.

She wanted to wrap her arms around him, comfort him, and for the first time saw him as something far more than a handsome, heart-stoppingly sexy man who was brilliant on the back of a bronc and a bull and who stirred her heart and other parts of her body. He was a man like she was a woman, strong yet sometimes weak, with a past of victories and defeats, joys and pains trailing behind them both.

"Me neither," she said, consciously pushing away the heavy heart thoughts of her mother always induced.

Kane had joined them, a plate full of barbeque chicken, baked beans, corn, and salad, balanced on his lap. His attention though was not on the food. She looked over her shoulder to see what had so completely captured Kane's attention. Oh. Kane fluidly stood to his feet and strode across the distance, his attention focused.

Luke made an irritated sound in the back of his throat. Unconsciously she put her hand over his as she saw Talon and Colt standing in line for Italian sodas made by the high school cheerleading team. Parker was perched atop Colt's shoulders and was talking animatedly to Tanner's neighbor and barrel racer Honey, whom Tanner had once mentored and now boarded her beautiful, championship horse, Halo. Honey wore a beautiful, white, embroidered western shirt and tight Wranglers.

Kane joined them easily, his smile dazzlingly and confident. He introduced himself to Honey, who fanned herself with her cowboy hat and then to Talon and Colt and Parker. Kane looked completely at ease. Talon had her fingers loosely around one of Parker's feet and she leaned into Colt and talked to Kane.

"C'mon." Tanner easily stood up, brushed a few crumbs from her jeans, and tugged Luke to his feet. "Time to stop playing ostrich."

"Ostrich? That's your best analogy? Can't I be compared to a more powerful animal?"

"Ostriches can be quite cool. They run fast."

"Running away is not a cool skill."

"Exactly. So don't run."

He took their two paper plates and tossed them into a trash can. "Tanner, really. This is not a good idea."

"It is."

"I need to focus for tomorrow."

"I know." She caught her bottom lip in her teeth and worried it, hoping she wasn't pushing too hard. "That's why you need to go over there like Kane did. Face it. Three brothers. Talking. Just for a few minutes."

For a moment she didn't think he would. His entire body radiated a barely leashed tension, and it was another hint that her cowboy—oh, how she wished he were hers—had far deeper depths than she had imagined.

"Please."

The nearly imperceptible easing of his tension gave her hope.

"It's not that I don't see a point to it." He took off his hat, looked at the inside, worried the brim through his hands and then put it back on again. "I feel like the timing is forced. He"—with a jerk of his head toward Colt—"doesn't want it. Kane's pulling out all his charm and the guy can barely tolerate him, barely stand still. Look at him. I can feel his tension and desire to cut out from here."

"But he's not." Tanner ran her hand lightly down Luke's spine, sensing Colt might or might not be uncomfortable with the idea of an instant family, and he certainly seemed like he'd embraced Parker, but Luke definitely was.

"Then let's go make it easier on both of them," she said, glad to think of a problem other than the possible bombshell her father had dropped this afternoon.

"No idea you were such a do-gooder, Ms. McTavish."

She smiled, still determined to lighten his mood. "I'm not. Total self-interest. In April, at the second annual bachelor auction, I spent a big chunk of my savings buying Colt for Talon, who's become a good friend this past year when she moved to Marietta. Now that he's left the army and they're engaged, I'd like to get to know him."

"This town has bachelor auctions?" Luke couldn't contain a laugh. "And the date works out in marriage? Why aren't dating sites shutting down the town?"

Tanner laughed. "Same thing happened last year so count yourself lucky you're here in September, cowboy. This town raises a lot of money to help people and causes. For example, the rodeo's steak dinner that you so kindly asked me to attend with you is raising money for Harry's House, a place for kids to hang out and do after-school activities in honor of Harry Monroe. He was a local boy and an EMT who was killed by a motorist on the highway a few weeks ago. He had stopped to help another motorist change a tire and was hit. Nicest guy. Nicest family. I went to school with him. I still can't believe it."

Luke slid his arm around her waist and she leaned into him for comfort. He felt so good. Strong. Warm. Alive. And sweet, kind, caring Harry was dead.

"Give your brother a chance. You never know what could happen, Luke."

The sudden image of him competing tomorrow rose up along with some of the sweet tea she'd drunk. Riding a bull was dangerous. So dangerous. He was good at it, but the best riders could be tossed and trampled. Secretly watching Luke compete from back stage when she didn't know him was going to be completely different from watching him tomorrow. A tremor quaked through her body.

"Hey." He stopped and turned, his hands on her shoulders, his body blocking out the crowd. "I'm going to be fine tomorrow." His voice was low and self-assured. "Better than fine. I'm going to ride whatever chance throws at me, and on

Sunday I'm going to win, and if you're there cheering me on, I might let you wear my buckle later."

"With just my boots and hat?" She said huskily, knowing he wanted to keep things PG, but that was so not where she wanted to go.

She was twenty-seven. She couldn't wait for what she wanted. Just like taking over for her father. She had to go with her gut and her vision. Not ask permission.

"Whoa, cowgirl, you're playing with fire."

She'd never said something so daring. So overtly sexual and Luke's eyes had gone molten gold, and it seemed as if their intensity branded her body with heat that licked along her skin and started a slow burn, deep and low. He loosely held her chin and tilted it up so his mouth was millimeters from hers. Her eyes drifted closed and her lips parted.

*Go for it.*

"And we never did get around to the licorice," she whispered against his lips. She breathed him in, and stood on tiptoes to capture his mouth. She wanted him to kiss her more than she wanted to breathe, but all she got was air.

Disappointed, her eyes opened and she saw him smiling a bit ruefully. "Audience," he said. "And you wanted us to go play nice in an Italian Soda line."

She bumped down to planet earth. It was probably for the best, but it sure didn't feel that way.

# Chapter Ten

TANNER PUSHED HER hat back from her face and blew at her damp face before jamming her hat back on and grabbing a wheelbarrow full of sawdust. She walked across the widest dirt aisle that separated the bull pens. It was a lot more crowded now with stock and handlers. Sawdust was thick in the air. Along with the clash of metal against hoof and shout-outs from caretakers.

She loved it all. The animals. The lifestyle. The dirt. The smells. The sounds. It was her world, but the man pacing so easily beside her had elevated her love of her job and the rodeo into a whole new realm of paradise. Luke was fun to be around, and he was so sexy he made it hard to concentrate.

They'd chatted longer than she'd anticipated with Luke's two brothers and Talon. It had been more natural than she'd expected although Colt hadn't done much talking but, according to Talon, he was usually fairly quiet unlike her. Parker, with his bottomless enthusiasm, had eased most of the strain. He had been so excited Colt was back for good and marrying his mom so he could be his daddy. He was also crazy about the rodeo and the fact he would now have two uncles who rode bulls. When Kane and Luke had each issued an invitation to give Parker a behind the scenes look, he'd been over the moon and would have tumbled off Colt's shoulders if Colt hadn't been built like Copper Mountain.

Talking with Talon and the three men had made Tanner wish she and her sister were closer. They used to be. Until her accident. It had taken her a long time to heal and adjust, and when finally she'd come home after months in the hospital and rehab, it seemed like her family had moved on without her. But maybe she'd drifted away, too. Tanner shoveled more sawdust than was necessary because the physical activity helped her cope with her racing thoughts. She'd been hurt they hadn't made an effort to visit after her dad came one time, and she'd been hurt later that Tucker made it so challenging to climb out of the background. That was Tanner's issue, not Tucker's. Tanner needed to be an adult and go for what she wanted, not just wish for it.

"Cowgirl, you shovel any more sawdust, you'll have to dig out those bulls in the morning." Luke held out his hand for the shovel.

She loved the small smile that quirked at the corners of his mouth. And the way his eyes glimmered behind their absurdly long lashes. What was the deal with men, real men honed in hard and dangerous work, getting the best eyelashes? Luke's would have been feminine if his face weren't so masculine.

She handed him the shovel and pushed the wheelbarrow off to the side, trying to think of what would be the best way to say what she wanted without being too vulnerable, without revealing… oh, screw it.

"You got a shower in your trailer, cowboy."

The way eyes lit up and his smile went full, Hollywood fantastic and curled her toes boosted her courage even further.

"I do," he said. "You want to see it."

"And use it." She pulled off her gloves and put them in her work bag that she hung on a peg outside the pens where her bulls were staying for the rodeo.

Then she subtly picked up a small duffle bag where she'd stashed a change of clothes and some toiletries in case she stayed with Luke longer than a quick hookup, before the walk of shame back to her truck, although she thought she'd be walking head held so high due to it being in the clouds.

He slid the bag off her shoulder and put it on his. Now that they were walking together back to his trailer, she felt a bit shy. It was one thing to be caught up in the moment like earlier today but quite another to pack an overnight bag. She fought the excuse to explain or to chicken out and by the time they'd reached his trailer, her heart was thumping so furiously she could barely swallow. Maybe she was being too daring. Tucker was just so much better with men.

"I can hear you thinking, Tanner." Luke stopped outside

his door. "Just jump in the shower. I'll stay out here and, if you'd prefer, we can head back to the street party after you've cleaned up."

"No. I'm not overthinking anything." She lied. "I just need a shower."

"Me, too, but ladies first." He unlocked his trailer door and pushed it open.

She walked in alone and made her way back to the small bathroom. Tanner shook her jeans out over the small, square shower and watched the dance of dust motes and sawdust drift down towards the drain. Then she carefully folded them. She did the same to her sky blue, western style shirt, wanting to keep the tile floor clean. His trailer was nice, lots of upgrades. Definitely nicer than the one she used when she traveled to the rodeo, and while the shower was small, it was nicer than her bathroom back at the Triple T. And the shampoo and shower gel smelled like him, fresh, spicy with a tang of citrus.

Naked, she turned on the water, but before stepping in she looked at herself in the full length mirror. She was being an idiot being nervous and self-conscious. She was pale and freckled but so what? She was healthy and strong, athletically slim and, while she had very small breasts, it wasn't like he couldn't tell just from looking at her what he was getting. She needed to stop comparing herself to her sister. Her dad had always done it. Classmates in high school, especially boys, had noted the difference, questioning aloud how she and Tucker could possibly be twins. But once she'd gone away to college, she'd been her own person, and coming home, shouldn't change the confidence she had built up over the years. She was a woman, not a young girl.

A soft knock on the sliding door interrupted her self-examination.

"Tanner, before you start, I have a clean towel for you."

His voice woke something hot and needy in her and banished the nerves. She remembered something Tucker had yelled at her once when she'd fallen off a horse while practicing one afternoon and had laid in the dirt a little too long. "YOLO!" You only live once. Wasn't that the truth?

Tanner slid open the door making no effort to hide.

"Wow." Luke made a sound at the back of his throat, and it seemed for a moment it was hard for him to breathe. Then he took a compulsive step forward, the towel dropping to the floor as he let go of it. "Look at you," he said and his hand shook a little as he touched her shoulder. "You're beautiful." His throat worked as he swallowed and Tanner felt her nerves settle and her confidence blossom. He looked awed, appreciative, not disappointed. "Luminous."

"That's a pretty word for pale, cowboy."

"Wow. Just. Wow." He breathed and with trembling fingers he caught the end of her braid and pulled out the elastic, then gently unbraided her hair.

His care and the reverence on his face moved her like nothing else, and she didn't even bother to blink back the unexpected sheen of tears. The real Luke far surpassed the Luke of her fantasies.

She tangled her fingers in his hair and began to back toward the shower pulling him with her just as she leaned up to close the distance between them. His kiss was hungry, way more assertive than when he'd kissed her earlier, or more accurately, she'd kissed him. He seemed all-in this time, and Tanner sighed happily and wrapped her arms around him, loving the press of the rough denim against her bare thighs, the dig of his shirt snaps against her chest and tummy.

He reached out to touch the water before it hit her and broke the kiss to dial it back. The gesture was so sweet that Tanner's fingers tightened compulsively on his shoulders, dug in and held on as if she could somehow keep him close for longer than one night.

The spray was warm, not hot and cascaded over her head forcing her to close her eyes, drowning out all sound except the swoosh of water, which concentrated all her senses into feeling Luke's mouth, his hands, his body. She had no desire to break contact so she dragged him all the way into the small shower stall with her.

He laughed and the vibration of his lips and breath against her mouth cranked up her desire. His shirt was slowly getting soaked and she popped the snaps and pulled, tugged, and peeled off the fabric, letting it slop down on the tile floor. Her hands reached out greedily to touch everything she exposed, savoring the muscle, hard planes, heated skin a little rougher than hers. Her mouth followed, closing over one of his nipples and flicking her tongue against it and drawing tiny concentric circles.

"God, Tanner." He moaned against her throat. "You're killing me." His voice was harsh and barely audible over the pound of the water.

She took that as encouragement and reached between them to cup him through his jeans. Her hand convulsively closed over his thick length.

"Tanner, wait." He covered her hand. "We… I have to…"

His voice strangled in his throat and she had no intention of waiting for anything.

She kissed him, and caressed him through his jeans and he pushed into her hand in rhythm with her strokes.

"Good?" she murmured, breaking the kiss slightly.

"God, yes." His voice shook. "Perfect," he said. "But we have to stop. I have to tell you something."

"Later." She angled his head down to hers and with one hand deftly popped his buckle and was started on the buttons of his jeans. She sank to her knees in search of treasure.

"Tanner." He caught her under her elbows and pulled her back up, held her against his chest. "I want to make love to you, but we need to talk first."

"Talk?" She blinked at him and then felt like the water went cold. Or was that her? "What about?" Men never wanted to talk. Not about anything good. And men never wanted to talk before sex and usually not after, although she wasn't anything close to an expert.

Her heart galloped and her breathing was fractured. What had she done wrong this time? She was naked and he was partially clothed, half undressed by her frantic and clumsy hands. She took a step back and he let her. Tanner felt it like a blow. Humiliating. But she hadn't made imagined the signs, had she?

"I'll let you finish up," he said. "And then we can talk."

# Chapter Eleven

TANNER WAS UP as usual at dawn despite the fact that there had been precious little sleep last night. She had been so embarrassed and then angry about Luke putting her off that if his trailer had had a back door or large enough window, she would have climbed out. Instead she'd finished her shower, dressed, and then walked back out into the main room to find Luke, Kane and his mother deep in conversation.

Silence and three pair of eyes had tracked her progress, and it had taken all of her willpower to not flush or bend under the scrutiny.

No classes on escaping awkward moments in college.

"Thanks for the shower," she said channeling an equal dose of perky and cavalier from a well she didn't know she'd dug.

Luke stood up and walked toward her. His golden gaze. His walk. Deadly to her restraint.

"I'll walk you out."

"I'm good," she said.

"I'm not," he said low in her ear.

Tired of feeling rejected, Tanner had turned around and stuck out her hand. "Tanner McTavish," she'd said to Luke's mother.

His mom had stood up, well, flowed really, all slim, graceful elegance with the same eyes as Kane, which was a bit spooky. She'd looked Tanner up and down, and Tanner felt lacking in all areas. Samara might have three grown sons, but she was beautiful and ethereal. Then she looked at Luke, clearly puzzled.

*Great. Obvious much*?

"Samara Wilder," she'd said her name, her intense gaze sweeping Tanner up and down. "You don't have to leave. You know Talon. You could help us get Colt to talk to me."

"Mom," Luke said.

Just the one word had shown so much, Tanner marveled. His exasperation. His love. His regret. His steel.

"I do have to leave," Tanner had said. On impulse she'd turned back to Luke and kissed him on his cheek. "See you tomorrow, cowboy. Hopefully you can hang on a bit better then."

Just to piss him off she'd winked at Kane, who'd openly laughed at his brother.

Tanner was trying to take the approach that Luke's sudden desire for a conversation instead of blood pumping frantic sex in his shower and hopefully other places in his trailer last night was for the best. Emphasis on trying. Still, today the rodeo opened and nothing, not even Luke Wilder, who was either the biggest tease or the most challenging man to read in her experience, could get her down for long.

The day of prelims was always busy, and since the Triple T was providing more than forty percent of the stock for this rodeo and two of the barrel racers boarded their horses with the ranch, Tanner was busy, but not so busy she hadn't had time to catch up with Luke when he brought her a latte as she worked.

She felt giddy, seeing him again.

"You found the Java Café." She breathed in the fragrance of an almond milk latte with a dash of cinnamon.

"Absolutely." He smiled, and Tanner had to restrain herself from kissing him because they had a major audience and she didn't trust his signals.

"And you brought my favorite."

"Small towns. I just said your name and the barista knew what you liked."

"Love my hometown." Tanner felt her tension from yesterday ease.

Luke was here smiling at her, and today was the prelims of rodeo competition and Marietta was getting a chance to shine for locals and tourists. Even the weather was cooperating.

"Will you get a bit of a break later?" he'd asked, leaning against the pens and watching her with his golden gaze that had permanently curled her toes.

"Don't you need to concentrate on your events?"

He didn't still want to have that talk, did he? Tanner didn't want to know. It was probably a deal-breaker like a girl friend or the let's-be-friends or I'm-not-ready-for-a-relationship talk. She'd heard it so many times before she could quote it. She so did not want to talk to Luke Wilder.

"I'm good." He made the move to her by sliding his arm around her waist and pulling her in for a gentle hug that left her in no doubt that he was ready. Instantly she felt her core heat. "Better than good."

Yes he was. Superb was a better adjective, but she was not falling into that trap again. Except she almost did as his eyes heated as they met hers.

His smile practically scorched her skin off.

"Maybe a walk?" His smile dimmed, and his eyes looked a bit sad.

She almost capitulated. Just get it over with. Pull the band aid. She ignored her higher self.

"You've only got a couple of hours before your roping events," she said, marveling at her cool professionalism. "And I've got bulls and horses to prep. I'll watch you ride. Hope you can stick it."

"Tanner McTavish." He straightened away from her. "I'm sticking the ride. I'm dancing with you tonight. I'm winning that buckle and the prize money. Don't doubt me."

"Talk's cheap. Show me," she said as he sauntered away. She could watch him walk for hours, but definitely the view walking towards was better than away.

Tanner watched at least some of each event in between work, but now that the bull riding preliminary rides were closing in, Tanner's tummy began to churn. What if Luke were tired? Distracted from his family's drama? She felt so anxious and sexually frustrated she was having a hard time holding on to her usual tools, ropes, pitch fork, shovels, everything. Her watch seemed to be ticking extra loudly, but she still kept looking at it, the time dragging when all she wanted to do was run off to find Luke.

"Hey, Tanner, Luke had his draw yet?" Kane was there, back stage pass clipped to a belt loop on his jeans.

She didn't bother to ask how he got back here. No one associated with the rodeo in several countries didn't know who Kane Wilder was. Nor would they deny him access to anything, any place, anywhere. She looked at her watch. Again.

"In half an hour," she said.

"Great." He leaned against one of the pen's posts, crossed his arms, and smiled at her.

Tanner blinked and looked away. Charm and charisma oozed from his pores. He wore confidence like she wore Wranglers.

"I hope you let him get a little rest last night." He teased.

Tanner's mouth opened and closed. "I have no say in his sleeping patterns," she said.

"Boy's losing his touch then."

And then like the mature scientist and businesswoman she was, she blushed fire engine red.

He laughed, cleft dimple on his chin prominent.

Oh, boy. He was lethal, piercing blue-grey eyes, killer smile with a dimple, thick, midnight black hair, long and wavy and casually caught back in a low pony tail, but he didn't move her the way Luke did. Too smooth, practiced. Calculating. She couldn't get a real read on him, whereas Luke had seemed genuine out of the chute. Self-contained, modest, kind. She practically sighed. Perfect. Luke was perfect. Not polished.

"You gonna give him riding tips?" She found herself irritated by the thought.

Kane laughed. "Hell, no. He's still my big brother. He might play nice, but he's kicked my ass too many times growing up for me to give him another excuse."

"Kept you in line, huh."

"Not enough, probably." Kane shot back, but the smile didn't reach his eyes.

"You close?"

Something flashed across Kane's face, but it was so fleeting she may have imagined it.

"We're brothers."

"You watch him ride a lot?" She asked curiously.

"Only after," he said.

"Why? Your schedules don't match?"

He was quiet a moment, looking down at his black cowboy boots that looked hand stitched, and for that split second, in the silence, Tanner felt that was the most honest glimpse of Kane she was ever going to get.

He looked up at her, and his blue-grey gaze seared through her as if trying to read her. Her chin notched up. Whatever he saw, it meant nothing to her. What she and Luke were, and it might, she thought with a painful twinge to her heart, be nothing, was between her and Luke, not his famous and wealthy brother.

"Luke's honest to the bone," he said, startling her.

"Non sequitur much?"

"Just saying."

He pushed himself away from the stock pen. "From what I've read about your breeding program and what I've seen on your ranch and here, the IBR would be lucky to have your bulls."

She couldn't stifle the rush of pleasure, and even though Luke was the stock rep, Kane Wilder's word would carry a lot of weight.

"That's Luke's call, but thank you. Wait. How did you see the ranch?"

"Your dad was quite happy to show me around. He talked at length about the bloodlines and pretty much let me look my fill."

His words were casual, but Tanner paused. "I would have shown you around after the rodeo," she said quickly, trying to keep her voice and breathing calm.

No. She was being paranoid. It would be too much of a coincidence that Kane had looked around her ranch and her father started talking about selling, wouldn't it?

"That's when Luke's going to spend a couple of days there."

"Oh. Is that what he'll be doing? Looking at the bulls?"

"Yes, the bulls," she said shortly. "And why are you trying to yank my chain? Why'd you go out to the Triple T without asking me?"

"Bruce McTavish is still listed as owner. Tanner McTavish is listed as a horse trainer and part-time animal husbandry assistant."

Tanner fought the urge to snort and roll her eyes like one of her horses. "That was years ago." She'd still been in school. "There's nothing part-time about me now," she said forcefully. "And why are you looking at my athletes anyway?"

He crossed his arms and looked down at her. She wasn't short at five-foot-eight in her boots, but Kane Wilder was tall for a bull rider, who usually tended to be built smaller as the lower center of gravity made it easier to stick their seat on the bull.

"Curious," he said, maddeningly vague.

She would have questioned him further, but he reached out with one finger and touched a wispy curl that had long ago strayed from her braid.

"You should wear your hair down more. I bet it's beautiful, like fire."

She jerked away from his touch.

His lips tilted in a smile. "Don't stress Luke out during a rodeo weekend."

How could she possibly stress him out? He was stressing her out.

"We just met," she said as casually as she could. It was true although it didn't feel like that at all.

"Sometimes time and people don't work like that."

*What the heck? Was he was a mind reader as well as international bull-riding super star? Fabulous.*

She fought her blush. He could not read her mind. He could not read her heart. He was fishing. Nosy brother with terrible timing. Prettier brother, her ass.

"I like the freckles. They suit." He leaned in a bit closer, which forced Tanner to take a step back, which she hated.

Hated! But no way was she touching Luke's brother. That would be weird, and she didn't like his game and was about to tell him so when his whole demeanor changed and went from playful to serious.

"Ah, here's Luke. Let's rock and roll."

Luke moved toward them, holding his gloves, custom bull ropes, and already wearing his chaps. She'd seen hundreds of cowboys wear chaps, but Luke in chaps stole her breath. His face was taut, his walk quick, purposefully eating up the distance.

"Hey," she said softly and was completely stunned when

he spanned one hand high between her shoulders blades and dragged her up against him and kissed her assertively.

Tanner stiffened momentarily, but the hard heat of his body and the insistence of his kiss had her forgetting Kane stood a few feet away and other cowboys and the stock teams were starting to gather in the area. She stood up on tiptoe and kissed him back letting her fingers caress his neck.

"Still here," Kane said behind them.

"And I'm wondering why," Luke said, slowly breaking the kiss.

He touched Tanner's cheek.

"Now that you've peed on a bush…" Kane said.

Luke's eyes narrowed and he swung around. "You can say whatever dumb ass thing you want to say to me. I've heard it all before, and I don't care, but not to Tanner. You can be polite and respectful or you can shut the hell up. Choose."

"Wait. What?" Tanner tangled her fingers into the fabric of Luke's shirt and looked from Luke to Kane. "Why are you trying to wind him up?" She demanded. "After your earlier stupid speech about me not stressing him out. Hypocrite. And you"—she looked away from Kane's grin to Luke, who looked tense and pissed—"what was that? Territory? Me? You're not… you don't think… We're not even…" She couldn't even get the words out.

He wasn't jealous was he? Please. That was dumber than dumb.

*As if!*

"Luke," she said, her fingers still gripping his shirt. It was a beautiful black silky western-style shirt that had a sheen and snaps with a bucking bull on them.

There was so much she wanted to say, wanted to ask, but when she looked into his eyes, shimmering with something that made her tummy flip and her heart beat ridiculously fast, like she was a young teen at her first professional rodeo again, she couldn't think coherently.

"I like when you say my name," he said softly, brushing his lips again over her mouth. "Don't forget, you promised to go with me to the steak dinner tonight."

"Yes." It was embarrassing how much having the date pleased her.

She traced his silver buckle, inlaid with turquoise and red coral. The buckle was engraved with mountains. He was going to ride in less than an hour where anything could happen. It was so stupid that she was so nervous she was totally losing it. She bred bulls to try to buck off men like Luke Wilder, and now she was terrified that he'd get thrown off—yeah, she who'd cheered each time her bulls had tossed a rider like a rag, even popped champagne with Josh and Jorge when their bulls maintained their one hundred percent standings.

"And you're going to dance with me?" He twirled one of her flyaway wispy curls around one finger.

"I love to dance."

"I know, I've seen you two-step with a rake and a shovel."

"I'm high in demand for dancing with barn tools."

"I want to see those skills later. Privately." He shot a dark look at his brother.

She heard the call for the cowboys to draw their bulls for the first round of competition.

Kane rubbed his hands together. "Hope you get a fuckin' fierce ride," he said.

And now she was a pervert who couldn't stop thinking about missing out on the fierce ride she'd wanted to give Luke last night. Talk her ass. There was nothing Luke could have said that would have changed her mind. Just thinking of touching him in the shower, having his hot, drenched heat grinding against her made Tanner bite the inside of her cheek and press her legs tightly together. She felt warm down there, damp.

This was ridiculous. She was a professional. She couldn't melt every time Luke walked up, picture him, beautiful and strong, thrusting into her body each time he walked by. And in the chaps. She was going to lose it. She was going to become the biggest buckle bunny ever after sneering at them for years. Only the only buckle she was interested in grabbing was Luke Wilder's. And if he were wearing chaps she would just die of pleasure at his feet.

"Catch you after," he said and kissed her cheek and looked at her, as if gauging her mood.

Like she'd be running away if he were anywhere close by.

"Yeah," she said, resisting the urge to grab his hand and hold on.

He headed away and Tanner was seized with dread. What if something bad happened? Even skilled riders could make a mistake, anticipate a move incorrectly, take an unlucky fall, get tangled in the grip. For a moment it was hard to breathe.

"Luke," she called out and ran toward him impulsively.

"What?" He looked so calm and focused she felt stupid.

She wanted to say what? *Don't go?* That was so dumb. The rodeo was a big chunk of his life as it was hers. If cowboys started being careful and staying home, she'd be out of business.

"Have a good ride," she said anticlimactically. "Stick it."

"Aren't you supposed to be rooting for the bull, cowgirl?"

"I just want that dance," she said cheekily.

"You'll get it. Glad you have your priorities straight."

"Always," she said, wishing it were true because she was definitely having a shift in her priorities, and she didn't think there was anything straight or smart about it.

Forty-five minutes later, Tanner supervised Twister being loaded into the chute and helped prepare him for his moment to shine. Twister looked in fighting form. He was an athletic, aggressive bull, who elevated and spun, changing directions seemingly in midair. He was one of the bulls she'd wanted Luke to look at for the IBR. Well, he was getting his look.

She was about to climb down the outside of the chute just as Luke finished his final stretches and adjusted his chaps, his gloves and damn he wasn't wearing a helmet. She knew he favored his hat. She'd thought it was stupid before. Sexy, but stupid, but now it was asinine, sheer idiocy. Kane wore a helmet. She knew because videos of his rides went viral.

She sucked in a deep breath. Men were not immortal, and she was lucky lightning didn't strike her for hypocrisy because she was fretting over a seasoned cowboy instead of focusing on her athlete's performance and score.

*Who was the idiot now?*

"Hey, cowgirl."

Tanner nearly lost her grip on the blue metal railing. She'd been so conscious of giving Luke space to get in whatever zone he needed to get into before his ride that she'd tried to keep from even looking at him so she wouldn't distract him.

She looked into his beautiful, warm, golden gaze and whispered a little prayer.

"Try to hang on." She teased. "And have fun."

"Always do."

She jumped to the ground and hurried around so she could watch through railing off to the side as she'd never be able to make it into the stands before he rode.

Luke's name was announced. Music blared. His stats were read off. He wasn't a local or well known on this circuit, but his annual stats definitely fired up the crowd. As did his All-around cowboy wins and two national championships. She was glad the announcer didn't say he was Kane Wilder's brother. Tanner counted her breaths waiting for the familiar slide of metal and hard hit of hooves on dirt. Eight seconds. For the first time in her life, she was not rooting for the bull. Luke was out, hand high, being spun around like he was on a demented carnival ride. Luke looked relaxed, but controlled as Twister lived up to his name and flung his massive body up in the air far more vertical than anything that size and weight should be able to.

The crowd was wild. The cheers and chants were deafening and swelled as the bell marked a complete ride.

Luke hopped off the bull as easily as celebrities slid out of limos to hit the red carpet. He took off his hat and briefly waved to the crowd, his eyes at all times on Twister, who strutted around, charging a few fences and glaring before being herded back towards the exit gate. For a moment Twister looked like he might charge again, but the whirl of the lasso near his head caused him to skitter sideways and then arrogantly toss his head before he ran down to the exit gate where he would be herded back to his pen.

Tanner should have hurried to make sure her bull got back safely and was checked out and given a treat, which she always did even though she had a full team in place, but she hesitated, her eyes on Luke as he retrieved his rope, looked at his score, and waved once more before clamoring easily over the fence and dropped down on the other side. He didn't seem injured or in pain or tired. And she was definitely on board with that.

"Yes," Tanner whispered, and was surprised to see that she was shaking.

She clasped her hands together. She had to get a grip. Luke was in town for the weekend and then a day or two to review her bulls, science and operations. She had to keep that thought fully in her frontal brain, which she had never before realized was so ditzy and sexualized.

"That was fucking awesome," Kane said bounding up behind her. "A thing of beauty. He made it look so easy. Classic. He's top on the score board."

Tanner had already figured that out, and her stomach flipped with excitement and pride, especially as she saw him walking toward them, slowed down by a lot of congratulations from various backstage team members and other cowboys. Even Jane Weiss from the chamber of commerce stood up on tiptoes to give him a quick hug and kiss on his cheek. He was clearly uninjured and feeling good, and Tanner felt a coil of tension release.

"Hey." He hugged her and brushed his warm mouth against hers.

"Hey, yourself," she suddenly felt shy.

"I know you're busy," he said softly. "Want to head over

to the steak dinner at six?"

"Sounds great." She tried to sound casual and only managed breathy, but it was her clue to get back to work and she took it.

He caught her hand as she turned to go. "You always look great, but if you want to shower, you can use mine."

"I'll keep that in mind, cowboy."

He held on to her hand. "Say my name."

She pressed her lips together. Somehow saying cowboy made it more casual, like she wasn't tumbling head over heels.

"I like it when you say my name."

"Luke," she said softly like she was committing to something far more intense and intimate than a steak dinner and dance.

# Chapter Twelve

NEVER HAD THE glowing, golden lights, woven within the trees of the park and stretched like a panoply of stars above the long tables, stage, and dance floor, been more romantic and beautiful to Tanner. She'd been here every year that she could remember, but this was the only time she'd had a date. And it was a date. She wasn't even trying to pretend it wasn't a date. She'd even bought a new sundress at a Marietta boutique during the entertainment break at the rodeo. And she was wearing her favorite vintage, tan ankle boots that were accented with embroidered flowers and beads.

She hated to miss any aspect of the rodeo, but seeing Luke's appreciative gleam in his golden eyes had been worth the effort. She'd fretted most of the afternoon but, in the end, had worn her hair partially down, pulled back from her face and wound in an elaborate braid but the back hung loose in a cloud of tight, red-orange curls.

"Gorgeous." Luke breathed in her ear as they walked into the park to join the festivities.

"Bit of an exaggeration, but I don't mind. Carry on."

The sun was setting, imbuing the park and the people in a rosy glow, and Tanner had to admit, she felt beautiful and happy and like she too was sparkling.

"You were saying, cowboy?"

"You don't deserve to know." He laughed, stopped walking and swung her around to face him, so her body brushed against his.

She felt his heat to her bones, and she caught her lower lip, unfamiliarly slicked with gloss between her teeth.

"I think it's time we were completely on a first name basis."

His thumbs feathered along her cheekbones, "Tanner?"

She could barely swallow around the flame of desire that ignited in her body and burned bright. She felt liquid. She felt clean. Strong. Like she was someone else. Powerful and passionate.

"Yes, Luke," she said softly.

And suddenly she wanted them to be away. She didn't want to waste the time mingling, eating, dancing. She'd been looking forward to spending the social time with him, showing him her town, her friends. Having someone by her side. Being a part of a couple even if it was only for the weekend. He looked so handsome in his black and gold checked shirt accented with black satin and black Stetson and black dress jeans.

"Maybe you aren't really hungry for steak," she said softly.

"Are you trying to get out of your promise of a dance?"

"There are different ways of dancing."

"Are you trying to seduce me, Tanner?"

"Yes. Is it working?"

"Definitely." He nearly brushed his lips against hers and then paused. "Oops. Don't want to spoil your makeup."

"Forget all that," she said and closed the distance between them.

She sighed as his lips teased hers apart. He kissed her gently and then took a small step back, but she followed, her hands sliding up his arms to his shoulders. She loved the way his body felt under her palms.

"Oh, no." He smiled and caught her roving hands. "You promised me a dance."

His smile knocked her sideways. "And a steak dinner."

He'd only kissed her, yet her heart was pounding and her breath felt tangled in her throat.

He must have noticed her flushed cheeks and elevated breathing because his golden eyes moved over her body with intent.

"Yeah, you should definitely get me fed so I have stamina for later activities."

The thrill that shot through her was visceral. It was also ridiculous. She was a woman, not a girl, but she hadn't flirted as a teen or in college. This was all new to her, and she loved it.

"I was nervous today watching you ride." She confided as they resumed walking across the park towards the buffet. "But you were so fierce and controlled. Beautiful to watch. You just dominated."

He slid his arm around her. "I'm not a roll. No need to butter me up. I'm pretty much a sure thing at this point."

The way he smiled, Tanner knew he meant to make her laugh only her heart pinched instead. She wished he were a sure thing not only for tonight but for longer.

*Always wanting more.*

Her mother had been like that. Look how that had turned out. She'd left a husband, who had adored her, and twin girls, heartbroken and bewildered. She'd even abandoned her cherished horse-breeding and training business. For what? What had she gotten out of it? Tanner never knew. Had it been worth it? Was her mother happy now? And how would Tanner find happiness again if her father sold the ranch, the business she'd built? Yes, she could go back to school, find another job on a ranch. But it wouldn't be home. But she'd cope. And she'd have to cope when Luke rode away as well, cherish the memory not mourn the loss.

"What is that quote? Don't be sad when it's over, be happy that it happened?"

"Why are you thinking about that?" Luke asked, startling Tanner because she hadn't realized she'd spoken aloud. "I am a lousy date if I'm making you philosophical." He caught her hips and did a quick two-step and spun her around in a tight circle.

"Smooth moves, cowboy." She smiled and looped her arms around his neck, emotion welling up, but she forced herself to not throw herself against him.

He tangled his hands in the loose part of her hair and tugged. "My name, Tanner."

And slam, the air was gone from her body. She felt like she was drowning in his liquid-gold eyes. He was anything but just a cowboy, but she had to admit she'd been protecting herself from the first moment. Steeling herself for when he walked away with a kiss and a smile and a thanks for the fun, because for Luke this might be a weekend hookup, but she'd admired him for a few years, and she didn't realize just how deep her crush had gone until she'd met the man behind the cowboy. He'd been far more fascinating, fun, kind, smart and sexy than even she had fantasized.

"Luke." Her voice broke.

"What's bothering you?" he asked, and the concern in his tone nearly undid her.

She was used to being the strong one, holding it together even when she was sad or scared or tired or insecure and even the thought of possibly sharing her weakness was terrifying.

"Hey, Tanner!" She swallowed hard as she heard her name called.

Luke swore softly but, for once, Tanner was glad of the distraction. She was in way over her head with Luke. She turned and saw Talon standing there.

"Colt saved you and Luke a seat, and it's strategically by the dessert table, which seemed like a good idea only Parker has discovered the lemon meringue mini tortes, so I need Luke's superior roping skills."

LUKE LAUGHED AS he was definitely not first on the leader board for roping today. Bull riding was another story. He and his bull had both pulled high scores, which if he could pull off again tomorrow for the finals meant he walked away with another first place this year. The points wouldn't be added to his yearly total on the Mountain circuit, but still, he'd have bragging rights, and he'd definitely be able to ride in the Copper Mountain Rodeo next year although no way was he going to stay away that long.

Tanner made him feel something he'd never felt before. Belonging. He felt part of something. Involved. Not just watching. And while he'd watched her bulls perform magnificently today, he wanted to come back to Marietta for more than business. And that should scare the hell out of him only it didn't.

Although he'd totally acted like a dick kissing her in the shower before he told her about knowing her sister. He'd intended to do the right thing, but when she'd flung open that bathroom door, totally naked and confident yet still a bit shy, his libido had just overridden his stupefied, very visual, very geared for sex brain.

He watched Tanner chat with Talon and a rodeo barrel rider improbably named Honey who'd had an amazing ride today and who also boarded her horse at the Triple T. Guilt niggled now that he was no longer in the throes of passion. Tanner was the total package. Brains. Beauty. Ambition. Compassion. Fun. She deserved the truth from him.

Should he tell her tonight?

She tilted her head back towards the sky and laughed and he felt something deep in his chest stir. For a moment it was hard to breathe. How was he going to tell her? And when he did, he could lose her. Lose her. The thought turned him to stone. He couldn't keep her. Could he? He wasn't built like that? He had no idea how to have a relationship. Had never seen a healthy one up close.

What was he doing? Tanner wasn't a casual sex partner. He couldn't treat her like all the other women he'd been with who had just wanted to hook a winning cowboy for the weekend. Tanner was unique. Special.

And he hadn't been completely honest with her. Yet.

So, full disclosure. He'd tried to talk to her last night, but his mother had arrived, and Tanner had quickly left. Now he was dreading talking about his history with Tucker even more. His stomach sank, appetite fled. He definitely had no lingering feelings for Tucker, but he suspected his blazing but brief fling with her wouldn't sit well with Tanner. It didn't sit well with him. He was a different man now, and what he wanted from life and what he wanted from a woman had changed.

He had to tell her. Tonight. But he soon realized that plan wasn't going to work and that window had closed. Tanner knew everyone and chatted with everyone. She looked so beautiful and happy. She just glowed and he felt awed to be at her side. He couldn't spoil her evening. And he didn't want to tell her in front of an audience.

Tomorrow he'd tell her. After his ride.

He shoved guilt aside and tried not to be so stupidly silent and tense around Colt, who was equally silent and tense, but Luke had a feeling Colt's silence was more of a permanent state. Kane, always in the thick of the action and drama made up for their lack in the conversation.

Finally as a group they sat at a long table, squeezed in together, and he was happy he was sitting next to Tanner only that didn't last as she stood up and greeted quite a few people. He loved watching the expressions chase across her animated face. Her liberal dusting of freckles made him imagine angels blowing celestial dust across her creamy skin, divining her as a unique and strong individual who took his breath away.

Feeling like he was staring like a lovestruck sixteen year old, he quickly got to his feet determined to do something—get drinks and rolls for their table, anything. He saw his grandfather on the other side of the park, leaning against several bales of hay that differentiated the picnic area from the rest of the park, talking with Tanner's father, both of them intense, clearly arguing. Colt followed his gaze and stood up at the same time to get lemonade.

Without speaking, they headed to the drinks area.

"Must be strange." Luke opened the conversation, determined to make more of an effort, as they weaved through people and tables to get to the drinks table where there were large metal jugs of ice tea, water, and lemonade. "Discovering an instant, but not fully functional family."

Colt didn't break stride. Luke didn't think he'd answer, and cursed himself for trying, as he'd told himself he'd let it be.

But as they filled up six glasses of lemonade for their group, Colt answered in a low, terse voice. "Talon's happy."

That always seemed to be the most important point for Colt. Talon. What would it be like to meet the right one and to know it? How had Colt shrugged off whatever past he had and embraced the idea of marriage and fatherhood so effortlessly while Luke felt he would make a mess of it?

"You?"

"I'll deal."

"You do the paternity test yet?" Luke asked.

He'd definitely shelved the request to focus on the rodeo and the Triple T bulls. Besides, now that the shock and instant denial had worn off, he felt like a test was moot. It wasn't like he had sex every night with a different woman. He would have remembered Jenna if he'd met her and had sex with her, even a one-night stand. He wasn't Kane.

Colt shrugged, and Luke noticed how fluidly he moved for a big man. He'd have made strong showings on a bull or bronco. He looked fearless. Fierce. Damn, genes were powerful things.

"Don't bother. Talon's changed her mind," he said as they walked back.

"Why?"

"She was…" He seemed to be searching for the right word. "She never had…" He stopped again. "She was thinking of Parker's future. That he might want closure when he was older."

"You don't think closure is important?" Luke asked, curious as to what made his brother tick.

"I don't give a fuck about shit like that. What's done is done."

Luke laughed. That was the truth.

"True." Luke said, remembering how hard his mom had worked for Kane's father to acknowledge Kane.

Kane didn't talk about his biological father, an esteemed orthopedic surgeon and lecturer in Scottsdale, but it didn't take a psych degree to know that even though Kane had graduated two years early with every scholastic award possible and had top test scores, he'd refused an Ivy League scholarship and embraced one of the sports most dangerous to bones, the early rejection by his biological father still burned hot.

"But we started the adoption paperwork and got our

marriage license, so I think she feels Parker is safe." Colt held four glasses easily with his long fingers and ate up the distance back to the table.

"You want to know about our dad?" Luke had to stand in front of Colt to stop his progress.

"No."

"Mom?"

"No point, but"—he didn't break eye contact—"Talon wants me to talk to her at some point."

He sounded as thrilled as if Talon wanted him to get a rectal exam.

"My mom, our mom, would love that," Luke said, shocked he was standing up for his mom who had caused him such angst and guilt over the years. "She'd like to explain. Tell you her story."

Colt shrugged off the offer of information, or family, and neatly shone the spotlight on Luke. "Not sure of your feelings and not asking, but Talon thinks her friend's in deep with you. She's worried."

Luke sucked in a breath. That had definitely been a warning, and he felt it like Colt's fist to his ribs two days ago.

"Hopes you might settle in Marietta."

"I never said—" Luke broke off, shocked by the realization that in some part of his brain the idea was not completely impossible. But still foreign.

They jostled through more locals towards their table.

"How did you do it?" he asked Colt, feeling lost for the

first time in his life. "Just jump in. Commit. Stay. Change the whole course of your life."

Golden brown eyes, so much like his own weighed him, and Luke felt like Colt saw it all. Everything Luke usually hid, pride, competitive streak, loneliness, resentment, restlessness that grew annually and he had no idea what to do with it. Luke waited, breath held like there really was some answer he could understand, use.

For the first time he thought he saw a ghost of a grin touch down briefly on Colt's mouth.

"I'm not stupid."

The three words hit like bullets.

The tall, icy glasses of lemonade chilled Luke's hands. Colt's words chilled his heart, but made him hyperaware of everything. The warm-up band finishing their tuning, sound check, and setup, people talking, flowing around them like bubbles around rocks in the Marietta River. Colt's eyes, eerily the same color as Luke's, the face so similar to his own. It was like staring in a damn mirror only he wasn't speaking the words.

"In Syria," Colt said, and a little of Luke's lemonade spilled as the casual statement sounded so exotic in the downtown park of a historical, but small, Montana town. A peek into his brother's past. His heart. "There's been a long drought. Years. It's quite desperate now, which is a partial reason for the unrest. Wells have dried up. Water diviners are called in and they walk the property drowsing with their angle rods visualizing the water they want to find. It's science and magic." He began to walk again.

"What's that mean?" Luke demanded, completely mystified. It was something his mom or Kane would have pulled out their asses that he was supposed to divine like some damn runes. Genes were a bitch. And why the hell was he falling for a geneticist?

Luke stopped in his tracks. Lemonade sloshed over his hands. Falling for Tanner. Fell for Tanner. Had fallen for Tanner.

"You look at Tanner the same way the water diviners look when they've found the spring."

LIFE WAS PRETTY perfect Luke was thinking after dinner as he and Tanner danced to another almost rock-laced country anthem by Tory Dixon of the band Bourbon and Boots. Tanner was flushed and her body was warm and pliant. Her smile was brighter than the moon that had risen to cast a glow to rival the golden glow of lights strung throughout the trees.

"I have a feeling we're going to be shutting this place down." Luke teased Tanner.

"I love dancing," she said. "But I never get asked."

"Why the hell not?" He demanded, pissed the cowboys and other men in this town were so stupid.

Although her voice had been matter of fact, he could see

a little hurt in her eyes. Not that he was going to give her up for some other stupid cowboy to lead across the makeshift dance floor.

"Well, first there was my sister, Tucker."

He winced guiltily. It was the first time she'd actually said her twin's name so he could no longer claim the excuse he hadn't known. Not that he would have but still a small escape hatch closed. He had to tell her. But, damn, Tucker had nothing, absolutely *nothing* on Tanner.

"Then because my injury took so long to heal, I was gone so long, I think people just think of me as this broken girl, and then because of all my schooling…" She shrugged, but didn't meet his eyes. "Might get a little intimidating as a lot of the ranch hands haven't done much college if any.

He caught her by her shoulders and pulled her into his body. She melted into him, and Luke wondered, almost dizzily, how he was going to let her go. She was everything he'd ever wanted, even when he'd been telling himself over and over he didn't want anything. Smart. Kind. Funny. A ranch girl, and so sexually responsive he felt like he'd somehow been sucked into a fantasy universe. Marietta was the last place he would have looked for happiness. He had his mother to thank for that, like so many other things she'd done that had irritated him at the time but had made him stronger, prepared for anything life threw at him.

He wanted to know everything about Tanner. Now. He kicked himself. He should know. How badly she'd been hurt. If anything still bothered her. And if he were being honest, he was beginning to wonder what more she wanted from life. Was there a place in it for a man like him?

That should have sent sirens screaming in his brain. Other than Kane, Luke was the last man he'd pick to go all family-man. But these past couple of days with Tanner had shown him a glimpse of a life he'd never thought he'd have much less wanted.

Colt's words came back to him. His challenging "I'm not stupid."

No. Colt wasn't.

But was Luke?

Probably. Stupid enough to want something he couldn't have.

The song changed to a soft, slow dreamy Miranda Lambert song, "Love is Looking for You Now", and Luke took the opportunity to pull Tanner all the way into his body, savoring the fit of her hips against his, the way her small waist fit in the span of his hands as he allowed himself the opportunity of touching her, savoring her warmth and floral fragrance. She'd worn a turquoise, strappy sundress so he let his fingers play on the long, slim, pale line of her back, wishing he could kiss each one of her freckles.

He nuzzled her neck, pressing a row of kisses up toward her ear. He felt the key to his brother's suite at the Graff in his back pocket. Kane had given it to him before dinner saying Luke might as well take advantage of the comfort and privacy and luxury. He'd declined repeatedly, but Kane would be Kane, forcing his will on Luke, convinced his ideas were always better. Luke always resisted, but maybe tonight he wouldn't.

He bet Tanner had never stayed the night in a five-star hotel. Hell, he hadn't except on a couple of trips with Kane, and while Luke had thought it a huge waste of money each time, he had enjoyed the over the top luxury and comfort.

"You smell like heaven and feel even better," he whispered in her ear. "And thank you for wearing your hair down." He allowed his fingers to briefly tangle in her cloud of silky curls.

Yes, he definitely wanted to see her beautiful hair and luminous body spread out on the no doubt, decadent thread count of the Graff sheets. To hell with sleep. He wanted to explore this woman all night, and for the next fifty years, if that was what he had left.

The thought should have freaked him out. Instead he felt certain, settled for the first time in his life. Not feeling the need to defend or be secretive in order to protect his choices. He remembered how Colt had spoken about Talon. Protective. Sure.

"I know I said we'd dance all night long," he murmured against her unglossed lips that parted almost instinctively to let him inside. "But my brother has offered to give up his suite at the Graff for us tonight if you'd like to join me."

"For real?" Her eyes, round with surprise, sparkled. "I've

only been in the lobby when I was volunteering as a Christmas elf last year. The hotel was rescued and refurbished and the lobby is beautiful. I can't imagine what the rooms look like."

He pulled out the key. "I can show you if you want. We can even be completely decadent and selfish heathens and order champagne and bill it to his room, which he definitely owes me for being such a pain in the ass little brother as he supposedly grew up."

"We couldn't," Tanner said, but the mischievous glint, coupled with the curiosity and longing in her expression, sealed the deal for Luke. He was for once going to take something Kane had freely offered.

"We could." He kissed her lips and felt like he was coming home so he deepened the kiss. "And we should."

He pulled her closer and let the music work its magic.

He totally missed the "could I cut in," until Tanner slid out of his arms and he found himself facing a smiling Tucker McTavish, her green eyes sparkling and red lips curved in a devilish smile.

"Well, look at you, Luke Wilder. You don't mind if I cut in, sis?" Tucker kissed Tanner on her cheek and then did a full body press to him so he could feel her curves, barely contained in a black and white sparkly dress that looked like it had been sprayed on her body.

He was so shocked he could only stare at her for a moment.

"You're supposed to say this is an unexpected pleasure, Tucker." She pouted beautifully and curved one hand possessively in his hair at his nape and the other around his waist.

*Totally unexpected.*

"And you're supposed to dance with me."

"I was dancing with Tanner."

"So I saw." She smiled up at him, dazzling. "And now you've got me." She looked up at him through her long black lashes. "In your arms again."

The "again" dropped like a bomb.

"Tucker, it was rude to cut in on me and your sister."

"I know about your IBR gig and I'm so proud of you, Luke, but really no one expects you to dance with Tanner all night. Besides it might injure her. The doctors said she would never fully recover from her accident. Besides, I saw you and I gotta say, Luke, the years have not only been kind they've truly gifted you. I don't remember all these muscles." Her hand slid down his back confidently.

"Tanner said she loved to dance." He was distracted by her last comment.

Had Tanner been hurting but hadn't wanted to let him know?

Tucker laid her head against his chest. "I heard you're in first place."

He tried to put some distance between them.

"Luke, you're not still mad about Cody, are you?"

"Cody?" Oh, yeah. The cowboy she'd cheated with. "No. That was years ago."

When the hell would the song end?

"Then dance, Luke Wilder. I haven't been home in a while and everyone is staring, and I don't want them to think something's wrong."

Shit. People were staring. He didn't want to be rude, but he also didn't like how she was touching him like nearly five years hadn't passed.

"No one's watching," he said easily. "And I'm just another cowboy."

That had hurt a long time ago, but now he wondered what he'd ever saw in Tucker. Yes, she was beautiful and her sex appeal consumed like a tidal wave, and she was funny, but she wasn't Tanner. And holding her like this felt all kinds of wrong.

"You were never just another cowboy, Luke Wilder. And that was the problem."

"Long time ago, Tucker. Water under the bridge."

"Not that long ago, and I'm in town the rest of the rodeo, maybe longer so we could…"

"No." He held her away from him, hands firm on her upper arms. Aware the music still played, he gently kissed her check. "No," he said again. "Absolutely not."

"As usual, my timing is perfect. I'm free to dance when the prettiest girl arrives to the dance," Kane said, coming up behind him, and Luke had never been so happy to see his brother. “This one can’t dance, am I right?” Kane inserted himself between him and Tucker, grinning his famous “I can sell thousands of products” grin.

“Kane Wilder.” He introduced himself to Tucker, whose narrowed, sparkling glare swung away from Luke and softened on Kane. “The better dancer.”

“And better cowboy,” Tucker said, smiling as he put his hand around her waist and swung her away.

“Damn straight,” Kane said, laughing. “See you around, big brother.”

Luke didn’t even wait to hear Kane’s taunt. He had a cowgirl to find and a lot of explaining to do.

# Chapter Thirteen

"HEY, SIS, SURPRISED to see me." Tucker jumped over a stack of hay bales and sat down next to Tanner who was sitting on the grass, facing the courthouse and leaning against the hay bales. The band was playing a Rascal Flatts song and Tucker tapped her foot to the beat.

"No text. No calls. Yeah, I'm surprised."

Tucker handed Tanner a glass of lemonade.

"Thanks," she said, looking her sister over. Her heart pinched a little and she mentally kicked herself. She always felt small that she envied her sister her beauty, her figure, her confidence in the world. She and Luke had looked movie star beautiful together. His fluid body and easy dancing had been well-matched by Tucker's grace, natural sensuality. And the way he had stared at her.

She had to admit it. She'd been jealous. An ugly trait, as was the bitter twin envy that had also reared its warty head as she'd watched her sister and Luke move effortlessly around the dance floor, Tucker smiling up into Luke's handsome face. He hadn't told her he'd met Tucker before. She swallowed hard, wanting to ask Tucker how she knew Luke but not quite having the nerve.

She took a deep drink of the lemonade hoping its icy sweetness would soothe her aching heart enough to go back to the dance to see if Luke was even looking for her. He must be. He was too polite to abandon her just because Tucker had flirted with him. Tanner was being immature, hiding over here. She used to sit here when she'd been a young girl, wishing the boys would ask her to dance, but they never had so she'd sit behind the hay bales and stare at the courthouse clock and the moon and listen to the music and pretend that was all she wanted from the evening.

Same as it ever was, a Talking Heads lyric rolled through her brain.

She choked.

Tucker laughed. "You didn't think I'd come here without whiskey. You need to kick it up a bit more." She slid her arm around Tanner's shoulders and pulled her tight. "Too much work. You're too thin, letting daddy's injuries run you into the ground. You know the work will never be done?"

"I love it though, Tucker. I'm all ranch."

Tucker scanned her face. "You liked college. You could go back. Be a professor. Teach. Work in a lab in Missoula or even the big city like Seattle or San Francisco. I love California. We could get an apartment together. I bet UCLA has a genetics program. Maybe you could even work on human genes. There must be more money in that."

"I'm happy here, T. Triple T is my home and my career. I love it. I do." She took another more cautious sip of the lemonade. "You never were subtle about spiking drinks."

"I was never subtle about anything." Tucker scuffed the pointy silver toe of her black boots, decorated with feathers and rhinestones in the grass.

"Why are you here? Because Daddy asked?"

"One reason," Tucker said evasively, sipping her lemonade.

"He's been begging you to come home for years. Begging you for visits every month."

Tanner took another sip and then put it aside. She had to face Luke. And her father. She didn't often drink whiskey and she'd been too excited and social to eat much dinner so she had to be cautious. Always cautious, she silently mocked herself unlike her more fun, glamorous sister.

"And the other reason?" She asked really wanting to ask about Luke, but not wanting to provide water or nutrition to the seeds of her jealousy and envy.

Tucker shrugged, not meeting her eyes. "Luke approach you?"

Tanner started, her mouth going dry. Here was her opening.

"I've contacted the IBR over the past year about having Triple T bulls considered for the IBR tiers. They've been earning higher scores, and stud fees are going up. Luke is an IBR representative. He showed up for the appointment."

She tried to keep her voice casual, but her stupid complexion gave her away. She could feel her face flush. Tucker looked at her and sighed as if Tanner were a disappointing child.

"You know he's Sam Wilder's grandson."

"Yeah." She'd speculated but seeing how Sam had slammed the gate on any possible family reunion that had been a definite answer.

"Montana's not Luke's territory. You ask why he showed up?"

"No." Tanner didn't like the way Tucker's tone. All know-it-all. Suspicious.

"Ask him."

"It doesn't matter. I don't care. He's the IBR rep."

"There's a rumor Whispering Wind's in trouble. Been in financial trouble for years. Whispering Winds borders our property on one side and suddenly Luke Wilder, who's never been to Marietta. shows up at our little podunk rodeo for the first time in forever, his mother and brother in tow."

"I don't like where you're going with this, Tucker," Tanner said. "It's like some Hollywood drama you're trying to cast yourself in. Luke's not like that at all."

Tucker sighed. "Get real, Tanner." Her green eyes searched Tanner's and she felt like pulling away, getting to her feet, and running from the sympathy that radiated from Tucker. "I get it. I do. Luke's real fine. God." She closed her eyes and licked her lips. "That man has some serious skills and his stamina, whoa. I couldn't walk right for a week and so didn't care, but I think he's here for more than IBR bulls."

"Wait!" Tanner struggled to her feet spilling her lemonade on the grass and splashing her bare legs as well as Tucker's boots. "You slept with Luke?"

"Hey." Tucker brushed at her legs and inspected her boots.

"Answer the question, Tucker."

"Well, we didn't exactly sleep," she said.

Tanner could barely hear her twin's answer through the blood pulsing through her brain, making her feel like an aneurism was imminent.

"You had sex with him?" Tanner's voice rose in disbelief, but already images of Luke, her Luke, although clearly he wasn't and never would be her Luke or her cowboy, swam sickly through her churning brain.

The way his face had looked when she she'd gripped him through his jeans, the way his mouth felt when he kissed her. Tucker had had all that and more.

Tanner couldn't catch her breath. She couldn't even see properly. It was like the world was going in and out of focus, fuzzy on the sides.

"You and Luke…" She couldn't get any more out, didn't know what to do with her body, couldn't turn the channel of her mind so she could think.

"Hell, yeah." Tucker stood up, smoothing the tight skirt

of her dress. "I wasn't going to pass up all that prime male meat," Tucker said. "No one would. Luke's hot and fantastic in bed. I thought he was the perfect hookup guy, but he wanted more than just a fling." She shrugged. "Possessive men are a bore. What's wrong with you? You're acting so strange."

Tanner looked around almost blindly. She had to go. But where? She didn't want to face anyone, especially Luke, and being in Tucker's smug, beautiful, confident, oblivious orbit was making her feel sick, like she was losing her mind. She didn't want anyone to have this kind of power over her. No one. Ever again. She'd been right to steer clear of men.

"Why do you care who I burn up sheets with anyway?" Tucker seemed completely unaware of the storm she'd brewed with her casual appraisal of Luke's sexual skills. "You've never been so judgey before. It's not like he's your type. Different town every weekend more than half the year. Be realistic, Tanner. You should see the buckle bunnies lining up at his trailer door. Typical cowboy."

*Didn't stop you from being one in a crowd.*

She wanted to hurl the insult at her sister who prided herself on being so special. So unique. No one could resist her. Tanner was going to throw up. For a moment she almost let herself. On her sister's custom boots, which had cost more probably than what Tanner paid herself a month since she was pouring as much money as she could back into the ranch.

But, no. She wouldn't give Tucker the satisfaction. Or herself the humiliation.

"Plus I don't trust his stated reason for being here. Triple T bulls have always been rodeo bulls. Suddenly IBR comes calling."

"You staying at the ranch?" Tanner icily demanded her twin.

"Was hoping I'd get a better offer."

Tanner swallowed the acid that had flooded her mouth and nearly choked on it. Head high she tried for casual or sassy but failed at both.

"Go check out, Luke. I'm sure you know which trailer is his."

"Maybe," Tanner said. "He sure looks fine, but after dancing with his IBR brother, maybe I'll try him."

"Fine." Tanner had no idea why she wasn't screaming at her sister, hurling things although drama had never been her style. "Catch you later. Make sure you say hi to Dad. He'll be thrilled."

Tanner jumped over the hay bale, hating how the impact jarred her pelvis, hating how it still ached some days when she was tired or it was cold, hating her limp and hating how she still was self-conscious about it. Hating Luke Wilder, but herself even more. Tucker was right. Luke Wilder was not Tanner's type.

Screw him. Screw all men. She marched back toward the festivities to tell Luke Wilder what she thought of him. She'd rather sleep on a cot near her bulls for the rest of her life than to open up her heart again. She was amazing with bulls, but she had lousy taste in men.

*Stick to your skill set.*

"Tanner, baby, I've been looking all over for you."

Luke's voice cut through her haze of hurt and thankfully only fanned the flames of anger.

"Why didn't you tell me you'd slept with my sister? No wait. How did she put it? Burned up the sheets. How'd you think of it? As fucking? You fucked my sister."

"Jesus, Tanner." Luke looked sick.

Good. She felt worse. "Then you were going to fuck me, but couldn't quite bring yourself to do it."

Luke looked shocked. She'd shocked herself. She never used that language before. Ever, and the word stuck in her throat.

"Tanner it was nothing like that." He swallowed hard.

"It was exactly like that. Why didn't you tell me about Tucker?"

He sucked in a deep breath, and her heart plummeted even as her stomach rose up to choke her. She realized then she'd held out hope that somehow he hadn't known or… she couldn't even think of another possibility.

"Tanner, please." He took a step toward her, hand out. "Let me explain. I—"

She held out her hand to ward him off and felt an unexpected urge to slap him. Hard. See her handprint on his right, perfect cheekbone to match the mark Colt had given him a couple of days ago. Was it only two days? How could a man get to her so quickly? What was wrong with her?

"Forget it. I don't even care."

"Tanner, I know I should have told you the minute I realized, but…"

"No." She grit out, interrupting him because if she let him speak, she'd weaken.

She knew she would. She was weak with him. He made her weak. Her voice shook as much as her hand and she hated, just hated that her eyes were burning with tears.

"Leave me alone."

She was not going to cry. She wouldn't. Tucker had helped her out. Again. Just like she'd proved her first boyfriend in college was a cheater. Tucker had had him naked in less than an hour after meeting him. She'd probably had Luke even faster. And would again. Tanner felt sick.

"Baby, it was years ago. Way before I met you," he said his voice rushed. "I didn't tell you because I didn't realize Tucker T was your sister until—" He stopped.

Her eyes narrowed. "Until what? She tossed me aside and you didn't give me a second thought as you spun her across the dance floor in front of the whole town?"

He'd asked her. But he'd danced off and stared dumbstruck at her sister in front of everyone. Cue the music. Same as it ever was, Tanner thought bitterly.

"It wasn't like that at all. Jesus. Can we talk about this

somewhere more privately?" He asked looking around, raking at his hair in frustration, his expression bleak.

Quite a few people were staring, including the biggest town gossip Carol Bingley, and for some reason that made Tanner want to make an even bigger scene. Why should she always be the ignored McTavish? Engendering sympathy? The good girl McTavish? To hell with all that. Why did Tucker get all the glory and power?

"No, cowboy. I'm not going anywhere with you. Ever."

"Tanner." His voice was tight. "Please. Please. Let me explain."

"That door closed when you knew she was my sister. When. Was. It?

He swallowed.

Tanner's knees nearly buckled, so she stood taller, straighter.

"Tanner, I know I should have said something the minute I realized. It was a dumb ass move. You're right to be pissed."

"We agree on that," she said tightly. "Now move. I'm leaving, and I don't want to see you again.

Colt had come up beside Luke.

"I would have appreciated honesty," she said, barely able to get the words out. "For once."

Each word was like an ice cube lodged in her throat. But she made herself meet his gaze, wanting him to know that she was serious and that she was not going to be played like a fool. She hadn't been a good-time buckle bunny, and he'd known it, but he'd taken advantage of her ignorance casually, without one iota of conscience.

But she was also not going to give up on her professional dreams.

"I hope you can strive for more professionalism and respect in your business dealings as an IBR stock rep." She spit each word at him. "And ask them to send someone else."

She had to get out of here because she was not going to be able to hold it together much longer. The rush of adrenalin and anger that had shot through her system had burned itself out, and now all she felt was stupid and humiliated and alone just like she'd felt when she'd heard her mother had left her family for good, and when her dad had told her he wouldn't be able to make more than one trip to Seattle Children's Hospital, leaving her far from home, family, and friends for months.

Abandoned.

But she had her bulls and her science and her goals. And that would be enough. It had to be enough.

"Tanner, you've got it all wrong." He tried to take her in his arms and his voice was low. "I told you we needed to talk in the shower."

She didn't hear the rest of what he said because there was a roar in her head like she was under water. And a pressure in her chest that hurt like she was cracking open. Her eyes burned. It mattered that he hadn't told her. That was character. And it also mattered that he'd been Tucker's. Her twin's words came back to mock her. Luke had amazing stamina. He'd wanted more than just a hookup.

"Please, Tanner, don't cry, baby. I can explain. Just calm down and talk about us."

"No," she said. "No talking." If he talked, she'd forgive him. She knew it, and she'd never forgive herself. "You're nothing like the man I thought you were." She said coldly, feeling each word drill into her bones. "Let go of me."

His hand was warm as he caught hers and for a moment she swayed, weak with longing. But then his touch was gone, and through her haze of tears she saw Colt jerking Luke away and then blocking him with his body.

"Get out of my way," Luke said in a deadly cold voice.

"She said 'let go.'"

"Fuck you." Luke growled. "I just want to talk to her."

"Walk away if you're going to go, Tanner."

Colt's cool tone chilled her to the bone and she felt a shiver of anxiety for Luke's safety, and that feeling was what decided her. She'd made a promise to herself as a teen when she'd been alone in the hospital for so many months to be strong, to be independent even as her life as she'd known it was over. To rebuild. To rely only on herself.

Tanner walked away.

"PULL YOURSELF TOGETHER," Kane said, voice as tight as his

features.

"I'm fine." Luke snapped. "Or I would have been fine if you'd let me talk to her." He glared at Colt, who leaned against the small fridge in his trailer, arms crossed, bulky body as rigid as a cedar trunk. "I didn't even know you existed three days ago and now you're interfering with my life."

He swore. Double teamed interference like he was some creepy stalker who was going to hunt Tanner down, which he would the minute he got rid of these assholes.

"She wouldn't even listen." He ground out, not meaning to say that out loud.

"There was nothing you could have said to bring that boat back to harbor." Colt said looking completely unaffected.

"Spare me the clichéd analogies. I thought you were army so why the stupid boat comment? Why not no bringing that bullet back to the chamber or gun or whatever?"

"I don't joke about shit like that."

"So that's you being a comedian? Stick to your day job." Luke groused, and then realized he didn't even know what Colt did now that he'd left the army—at least Luke thought Colt had.

Luke's fingers flexed reflexively and he balled his fists, willing them to stay locked at his side. He wanted to hit Colt for interfering. And hit Kane for demanding this dumb ass powwow in his trailer. His space. And Tanner hadn't answered his texts or calls and he really, really needed to see her. To reassure her that what had happened with Tucker had been a lifetime ago. That his brief affair with Tucker had been nothing more than a blip in his life, whereas Tanner… he walked another tight circle around his trailer, hating his brothers. Hating his own stupidity for wanting to wait to tell her until after his last ride. Tucker was his past. Nothing to do with his feelings. Tanner was his future.

Only maybe she wasn't.

A soft burr of a cell text had his heart leaping into his throat, but it was Colt's phone.

"Talon's ready to go home," he said, straightening from his lazy pose against the fridge. "Parker's tired. You good?" he asked Kane, which pissed Luke off. Like he was someone they needed to watch over.

Kane looked at Luke. What the hell did they think he was going to do? Rampage through the town? Start a fight at the Wolf Den? Have sex with the first drunk buckle bunny who said "hi?"

"I'm pissed," Luke said aware he sounded like a bratty teen so he tried to dial it back so both would get the hell out of there and he could figure out his next move.

Despair swept through him, but he shut it down. God knew what Tucker had said to Tanner because obviously she'd found Tanner before he had and had deliberately poured a pound of salt into that wound.

"Take them home." Luke pinched his nose and shut his

eyes, willing away the vision of Tanner's soft green eyes sharp with pain.

He knew she'd felt eclipsed by her sexily flamboyant and self-centered sister over the years and now he'd contributed to that pain in a very public but inadvertent way. He wanted to hold her. He wanted to tell her how much she meant to him. That seeing her smile was more beautiful than any sunrise. Damn, he was getting stupidly poetic.

"See you tomorrow." He tried not to say it like a curse.

Colt nodded. He left the trailer so quietly Luke had to look up from his contemplation of the wood floor Kane had had installed to make sure he'd truly left.

"I don't want to ask again," Kane said. "Are you going to be able to have a clear head to ride tomorrow?"

"I'm not a big stadium draw like you." Luke drawled. "But I'm not an amateur."

"Cut the crap and stop feeling sorry for yourself. You brought this on. You'll fix it."

"I was trying to fix it, and stop acting so smug. Just wait until one of your past mistakes rises up and fucks up your future." Luke couldn't help the bitterness in his voice.

Kane, usually quick with a self-satisfied come back, was silent, and Luke, despite his emotional turmoil looked up.

"Is she your one?" Kane demanded.

Luke wanted to laugh off his brother's hippy-dippy comment. Kane meditated twice daily and did so much yoga he should probably run his own ashram. Only Luke didn't feel like laughing. And it would be disrespectful to Tanner.

He sighed heavily, ran his fingers through his hair and walked again around the trailer, unable to stay still. "I've only known her a few days, but—" He broke off.

*Fuck it.* Honestly was the best policy. If he'd been upfront from the moment Kane had told him who Tucker T was, he wouldn't be in this situation. Or maybe he would be, but at least he wouldn't feel like a douche.

Probably like his biological father had been over and over again.

"She feels right. We fit. I really like her."

"That's a ringing endorsement."

He flipped off Kane. Typical for him not to get it. Not to get Luke.

"Liking a woman. Enjoying her company is as important as love and sex," he said. "You ever like a woman?"

"I've liked plenty of women."

"No. I mean really liked. Wanted to spend time with her talking, hanging out, because she makes you laugh, makes even everyday things like going to the grocery store or planning dinner or catching a movie fun, special. You notice and are fascinated by little things, like the line of her nose in profile or the way the sunlight plays in her eyes, making them look like sparkling pebbles in a stream one moment, new spring, birch leaves the next. You feel what she feels. You want what she wants? Her goals are as meaningful to you as yours are."

He shut up. Waited for Kane to mock him for being a failed, clichéd, cheesy poet. He and Kane hadn't had heart-to-hearts over the years so why was Luke trying now, especially when his stomach was in knots? His head felt like it was being squeezed in a vise and his skin felt like it would split open if he couldn't talk to Tanner, take the pain and betrayal from her stark face.

"Yeah." Kane shocked him by admitting. "And I fucked that up pretty spectacularly as well." He laughed without a smidge of humor. "Brothers. Genetics."

"Blood's blood." Luke echoed Sam Wilder again.

Luke could barely wrap his head around the concept of Kane fucking up anything. He'd always been golden with his mom, teachers, neighbors, classmates, girls, rodeo coaches, friends' parents. Everyone had loved Kane. He'd been the fun, smooth, charming, easygoing guy. Luke had always been so earnest. Responsible. Detailed. Practical. Dull.

"Who?"

Kane brooded.

"How? You've never blown anything in your life."

"The usual way."

Luke didn't know what to say, what to ask next, but judging by his brother's unexpected bleak expression, he wasn't sure he wanted to know. But Kane's usual way was sex.

"You thinking of Sky?" He finally asked.

He'd never known what had happened after Kane's best

friend growing up, Wit Gordon, had died in a freak rodeo accident during training. Kane hadn't talked about it much. They'd lived apart by the time it had happened, but he'd always expected that Kane, who'd always been protective of and close with Wit's younger sister, would eventually marry that girl only Kane had proceeded to build as massive a reputation for riding as many women as he had bulls.

"Yeah." Now it was Kane's turn to be restless as he prowled around the trailer.

Man, he needed a bigger rig or they both needed to take a long run. Nothing else but talking with Tanner would have the power to even begin to settle his head.

He didn't press for more. He had an imagination and he knew his brother and how he worked and Sky had been a beautiful and unusual child and as a teen, the last Luke had seen her, she'd been probably one of the most beautiful and ethereal women he'd ever seen. The way she moved, like a silk scarf blowing in a gentle, afternoon Montana breeze was both breath-catching and sensual. As a child, Sky had been a pest, following Kane and her brother everywhere she could, and teenage Sky had been fixated and obsessed with Kane to an almost embarrassingly degree. So, no, Luke didn't need a crystal ball to know what had happened and why Kane hadn't let it happen again and why Sky probably wasn't talking to him anymore.

"Sex has caused more problems than it cures." Luke diagnosed morosely, thinking if he'd kept his hands to himself like he'd initially intended and instead had just talked to Tanner, he'd probably be inside her paradise right now instead of banished to hell. But, damn. She was the one who had answered the door naked, wrapped her long, slim legs around his waist. How was he supposed to resist that?

On cue, two sharp knocks on his door startled him. He leapt to open the door, careful not to fling it open in case he hit Tanner with his enthusiasm.

Only it was Tucker smiling up at him, a flask of whiskey now nestled in her cleavage, which was now so avidly on display he could see her pale pink nipples peeking up at him.

*Fucking fabulous.*

He exerted rigid control of his limbs and clenched his jaw because every impulse screamed to slam the door and lock it, and every word that hurtled through his brain was mean and nasty, when his anger was really directed inward because he'd not been as open and honest with Tanner as he should have been.

"Good evening, boys. Two for the price of one." She smiled and slid the flask out of her cleavage. "I saved some for you. Two Wilders have featured in many of my wilder dreams."

Luke barely managed to not roll his eyes. Kane came to the rescue.

"Hey, Tucker T. I enjoyed our dance."

"I heard you were the wilder Wilder." Her gaze traveled down his body and then centered on his crotch. "Is that true?"

"No."

"Modest. Twosome?"

"With my brother, not a chance," Kane said. "But how 'bout I take you home."

"Forget it. My dad said 'too little too late', whatever the hell that means."

"That means I'll take you somewhere else," Kane said easily and held out his hand towards Luke.

"What?" Luke stared at Tucker in dismay.

He'd dealt with many drunken friends and lots of drunk women over the years but this one was TNT. And he did not want to be seen anywhere near her, especially spilling out of her clothes.

"Key. You have my room key still."

"You can't take her there. She's drunk." He mouthed as if it weren't completely obvious.

"You want to have her sleep it off here?"

Luke shoved the key in his brother's hand. "Hey, she's not—"

"She's right here and she's fine," Tucker said. "Totally consenting, so you don't need to act like idiot boy scouts with a moral compass the size of a sundial, but she is more than a little pissed off at life, my dad, my sister, and boring men who didn't used to be so boring and uptight. Oh. And paparazzi, who didn't even get my name right. Assholes. Oh, yeah, and my agent. And that damn director who thinks he's all that. And Hollywood executives, if you really want to know. And married men suck the worst. And that's just for a start." She rambled.

Luke's list of things he was pissed off at was plenty long without listening to any of hers.

"You're just going to put her to bed, right. On her own?"

"Jesus." Kane shook his head. "One day you and I really need to have a heart-to-heart."

"Now that sounds more promising." Tucker tangled her fingers in Kane's shirt. "God your chest is like granite. I want to see it."

Kane caught her fingers. "Could use some help," he said to Luke.

Luke held up his hands. "I'm already in trouble about something I did years ago. Go get some help from the Triple T crew. They are set up by—"

"I'm not going public with this," Kane said. "She'll be sober in the morning. Fine. I'll go it alone. Won't be the first woman I've taken home or to a hotel room to sleep it off. Alone." He added. "And then had my name splashed about as doing something else although I would have hoped my brother would have known me better." His voice was heavily sarcastic at the end enough that even Tucker, starting to stumble a little, noticed.

"Siblings suck," she said.

"Some days," Kane agreed as he led her out of the trailer. He turned at the end. "Get some fucking sleep and don't try to talk to her until the morning when she's calmed down. If you don't, I'm going to pull your name out of the finals myself."

Luke kicked the door shut. Locked it. Definitely, siblings sucked. Big time.

# Chapter Fourteen

TANNER DECIDED SHE hated the dawn, especially when she hadn't slept. And she hated reasonable friends who held her when she cried instead of compiling a list of why Luke Wilder was the biggest jerk on the planet. Instead, after all the tears had dried and her headache had pulsed like a disco beat, Talon had made Tanner a nonalcoholic smoothie with two crushed up Tylenol PM and told her she had to talk to Luke in the morning before he rode. She owed him. Talon had actually said that. Tanner owed him a chance to explain.

And now Luke's brother strode up to her all grim and humming energy as she shoveled fresh sawdust into each of her bull's pens, even though Jorge had cleaned everything out last night, and she'd done it again this morning, just because she couldn't stand still or think. She'd start crying again like the biggest whiney girl ever.

"You talk to Luke yet?"

"Not my priority." She snapped, her headache still a vivid memory, her throat dry, and her mind sluggish from the

Tylenol because it hadn't worn off so she felt hung over with no alcohol or fun memories to counteract the morning after.

"Make it your priority." Kane grabbed the shovel out of her hand.

"Hey." She grabbed it back and engaged in a useless tug of war.

"Hey, yourself. You can't let him get on a bull like that. He's losing his goddamn mind. You know what could happen."

Tanner swallowed hard, the fight bleeding out of her as fast as her attitude, but she tried to grab it back so she could keep some control over her battered heart.

"He's a big boy. He can make his own decisions."

She didn't tell him Luke had gone to the ranch last night looking for her, earning her a pissed off call from her dad who'd been woken up. Then Luke had woken up Jorge, who also wasn't happy with her. Then he'd staked out the bulls this morning until the rodeo grounds staff had made him leave since he would be competing that day and couldn't hang out around the bulls. The whole time she'd been crouched behind a wheelbarrow like she was a four-year-old in trouble.

"You like him?"

"He lied to me."

"He didn't lie."

"Pretty enormous lie by omission."

"That's true. Let Luke explain."

"Thought that's what he was trying to do by sending his so-called prettier little brother."

"Not that shit again. I'll kill him if he used the word prettier at any point."

"Be my guest."

"I know it sucked that he was, uh, with your sister, but it was four or five years ago. He didn't even know you. And Luke can't handle drama. Really sucks at it. Our mom should have been a soap opera star for real. She did a number on him growing up, and he handled it all so I didn't have to."

"I'll buy him a violin."

Tanner wanted to yell at Kane that Luke had met her first. Twice. Sort of. And that she'd noticed him more than five years ago. That she deliberately took her bulls to the Mountain circuit rodeos just so she could watch him ride. It would be too pathetic. She was pathetic. But they had been introduced. At two sponsor events. He'd shook her hand and said hi and then had moved on, his beautiful golden eyes drifting over her vaguely to land on the next person in the group.

"This isn't even about Luke and you know it."

Kane's words were a slap in her face.

"So what? Your sister was prettier than you. Don't load him up with your crap before a ride. Carry it yourself. You're a big girl. You talk to him or I tell the judges he's compromised and can't ride."

"You can't do that." Tanner breathed. "He'd never forgive you. He's in first place by eleven points."

"I don't give a fuck how many points. Won't matter if he's distracted and thrown. Trampled. Gored. You of all people know what can happen when a ride goes south."

Tanner could barely breathe as images of Luke, his beautiful face taking a full errant hoof, or his—the images made her sick and she bent over, holding her stomach.

"Then what? You'd feel bad? Wished you let him explain his feelings. Why he did what he did because he sure as hell had a reason for waiting to tell you about Tucker. That was years ago. Not this weekend. You need whatever the saying women have for balls to listen instead of hiding away like a little girl nursing hurt feelings from a decade ago. Only it's too late to talk if he's dead or fucking brain damaged because you were a coward."

Tanner held her hand palm out. He had to shut up. It was enough. The images were brutal and he was right. Talon had told her the same thing only more gently.

"You're right." She stood up, feeling bruised around the middle only he hadn't come within a few feet of her but his energy swarmed around him, buzzing like a displaced hive of bees. "I should have let him explain. I will. I promise."

Kane continued to stare at her, his pale grey eyes almost swirling silver with emotion. His face tight with anger. His body, longer than Luke's but just as rangy and hard, tense as a pole.

"You're right." She repeated. "Before the ride. What?" She demanded as he continued to stare, his pale blue grey eyes so intense she felt as if her skin would peel off.

"Trying to see what he sees in you," Kane said his words, another left hook, and Tanner flinched.

She'd wondered the same thing. She hadn't been able to believe it, and now his beautiful and famous brother was confirming all her worst fears.

"He's always held himself apart from everyone. Never let anyone close. I want to know why he finds you so special because he doesn't seem very special to you."

Tanner didn't even think. She lunged forward, her fist a blur as she slugged him in his hateful smug mouth, managing to pull the punch just slightly at the end as her brain kicked in even as the words spilled out. "You don't know me. You don't know my heart!"

She sucked in a shocked breath, holding her fist like she could take it back. She looked at his lip, split and swelling, a trickle of blood, and then he smiled, the famous smile she'd seen on dozens of rodeo products and she saw all his teeth, thank God. He probably had insurance on that famous smile. What the hell had she just done? She hadn't hit anyone since second grade when Tommy Applebaum had continued to taunt her with the uninspired "carrottop."

"I do now, little girl. Time to grow up."

And he turned and walked away, fluid and cocky, and Tanner just stared at him, her emotions jumbled and her thoughts and body feeling definitely off-balance like the world had just tilted a few degrees. Had she just been played? By another Wilder?

AS THE MORNING wore on, Tanner's courage hadn't failed her so much as fate. A bull from another contractor, Wicked, had escaped his handlers and then stampeded down two aisles of holding pens before being cornered by a swaggering cowboy on a beautiful, black horse, wielding a lasso like he was in an old time western movie. The problem? The bull was clearly in pain about something and the Triple T bull involved in the fracas, Spiral, named by Jorje's ten-year-old son because as a calf he used to spin in tight circles like a cat chasing its tail, had slammed himself against his gate and had gouged his rump on something. The bleeding wasn't bad, but Tanner wasn't taking any chances. Noah Sullivan, the large animal vet on call this weekend was busy with Wicked so Talon had climbed up on top of the pen, wielding two syringes, and cleaned the wound while Jorge and a new ranch hand, Evan, controlled Spiral. She dosed the bull with antibiotics, and numbing medicine and then stitched the circular gouge closed.

"Remind me why you're in school?" Tanner demanded.

"So I can get paid," Talon said, watching Spiral critically. "I only know how to do all this because I've stalked Noah relentlessly and he's let me, and I read all the time."

"Not all the time." Tanner teased, trying to find her inner friend and professional instead of the anxious woman afraid to have her heart broken by a cowboy she had a bad feeling she'd fallen in love with while she'd been wasting her time worrying that she was starting to like Luke too much.

"I'm not kissing and telling," Talon said primly, but her fair complexion couldn't hide the blush and her beautiful blue eyes shone with happiness.

Tanner caught her breath. She'd always thought her friend was pretty, with an inner kindness and strength that radiated, making her beautiful. Tanner realized that was how Luke had made her feel, like attraction wasn't just physical but soul deep, and she had ignored that for some hurt that had been born long ago in her childhood. Kane was right. Time to grow up.

Tucker had always received more of her mom's attention because she was so pretty and girlie; her father had always favored Tucker because she knew how to play him where as Tanner had always separated herself, trying to outwork and out compete everyone. And in college she'd been in a more male-dominated field, just like ranching, and she still tried to outwork, out compete everyone like she had to prove her worth instead of just enjoying her accomplishments and enjoying everyone around her.

As if reading her mind, Talon looked up, sympathy stamped on her face. "Did you talk to Luke yet?"

"No." She stubbed her toe in the dirt.

Around them fluttered rodeo life—smells of animals, mixed with popcorn and grilled hotdogs and hamburgers, snuffles of livestock, chatting between their handlers, and, dimly, the rodeo announcer and clapping, cheering, and foot stomping on the metal bleachers from the crowd soaking in the entire experience. Tanner loved it all, but today her heart was heavy, not interested in engaging with the crowd and the events.

She knew if Luke were here, she'd want to watch him prepare for his ride, maybe share a quick snack at one of the food booths. Or maybe they would have enjoyed pancakes at the annual pancake breakfast in Crawford County Park, a Sunday tradition for as long as she could remember. Today was the first one she'd missed.

"Last night I felt so betrayed," she said. "I still do even though it's probably not the right feeling."

"Feelings aren't right or wrong," Talon said. "They just are, but not opening up and sharing where the feeling is coming from, that's harmful. If you want to build something with Luke or someone else, you have to let them in, really in."

Tanner sucked in a deep breath. That was it, wasn't it. She didn't want to be that hurt little girl again, vulnerable. Abandoned by her mother, feeling abandoned by her father and her sister after her accident, remaking her life and shutting her family out of it, deliberately becoming as unlike Tucker as she could, no longer confiding in her, and not confiding in her father.

Oh, she'd been the good girl, coming home, leaving school after he'd been hurt in an accident, but she'd taken over the ranch, deliberately and methodically changing things, remaking the ranch into what she wanted rather than asking his opinion, and now that he felt well enough to do more, she kept trying to sideline him. Why? So she'd have the power. So she wouldn't be hurt.

"You make it sound so easy," she said, not sure she liked herself after all these revelations.

Kane hadn't been exaggerating. She had been running scared. A coward. She tasted the word in her mouth. Bitter. Metallic. Foreign.

"Not easy. But worth it. Colt is the first to say he sucks at communicating, but I push and push and we're getting there, but he speaks more with actions, not words so I have to learn his language, and I sometimes overwhelm him with… well, with mine, with me." She laughed. "I talk a lot, ask a million questions, share everything so he has to learn my language. But totally worth the risk. Really."

"You could be an advertisement for love. The perfect couple," Tanner said, remembering how she'd shown up at their small ranch house last night, when she'd been unable to stand her own company anymore and hadn't known what to do with everything burbling up inside her. She'd felt lost.

Colt had answered the door without comment. Had made her a hot chocolate with a large splash of brandy, handed it to her, and steered her toward the couch in the living room and draped a blanket over her in total silence while Talon had dressed and popped a quick batch of chocolate chip cookies into the oven. Never once had either of them made her feel like she was overreacting or interrupting when, obviously, she'd been doing both.

"He's definitely perfect for me. I love how he's so all-in with everything in our lives—starting a new career, learning to build barns at a place out towards Livingston and working at Big Z's sometimes, parenting Parker, supporting me while I'm in school. He never leaves me in doubt. I can totally rely that he will always try to do his best for our family, but no, Tanner, it's not easy. Sometimes I wake up at night and he's on the porch just staring. Or on the roof just sitting up there. Or out in one of the barns with his punching bags just hitting and kicking in this wild, raw fury, and he won't talk, and I have to let him be until he comes back to me, but it's totally worth it. Colt's worth the effort for me. And I'm worth the effort for him. You just have to figure out if Luke is worth the effort for you."

The instinctual "yes" she said startled her.

"Then talk to him." Talon swung off the top of Spiral's pen easily and Tanner admired her efficiency and grace. "Tell him how you feel. He can't be a better partner if you don't tell him what you need and what you want."

"He's going to think I'm some drama queen." Tanner groused, and she knew he hated drama, but she'd already decided she was going to suck up her pride and hurt and get back on her adult horse, so to speak.

"Everyone deserves a brush with royalty now and then." Talon teased, then she looked at her phone, which buzzed with a text. "Noah's going to be another thirty minutes or so with Wicked. You probably want to watch Honey and Halo nail first place in the barrel racing event."

"Yes, let's do that."

Only they didn't. Tanner had just settled beside Colt and Parker, who was loaded down with a bucket of popcorn and cotton candy, which he cheerfully broke off a chunk with his grubby boy paws and handed to her with a pink candy mouth, gums and teeth grin, when Honey was announced. They stood and cheered. Parker so wildly that Colt wrapped his hand around the kid.

"Hey, Halo!" Parker yelled over the announcer's voice.

He must have felt invested in Halo and Honey's potential win because every time he visited the ranch with his mom, whether it was official or unofficial, Parker would greet each horse by name and give them a small treat—an apple or carrot or handful of oats.

"Yes!" She shouted as Honey and Halo took off, form and stride perfect until Halo stumbled badly and Honey tumbled off. It happened so fast it took the crowd a moment to react, but not Tanner. She was already up on her feet, sliding through the railings and dropping a bit too far down to the dirt and grass below, but she ignored the jar to her joints.

"Tanner, get back." One of the cowboys was attempting to lasso Halo, who easily ducked the rope twice and remained by Honey's still side clearly agitated, stamping, whinnying, her hooves too close to Honey's prone body. Halo got increasingly agitated when the cowboy prepared for another try.

"Hold off a second, Jarod," Tanner said.

She stared at the Halo's hooves, feeling sick to her stomach. She'd been on the receiving end of those more than once, but she couldn't help Honey. She had to focus on her job—Halo, because once she got Halo under control, the EMTs could get to Honey. She could see them hovering at the gate, medical box and stretcher in hand. So strange not to see Harry Monroe there, but she pushed that awful event out of her mind as well.

She began to sing and Halo looked at her, watched her, eyes rolling, huffing, shying away nervously but not running, not stomping. Tanner kept her eyes a little lowered, arms loose at her sides, but she continued to approach slowly, talking softly, singing a little bit.

"Hey, Halo. Good girl. Look at you. Halo, sweet girl."

"You think you can catch her before she bolts," the cowboy asked, voice and rope lowered.

"Yeah. I'll get her."

Tanner focused on the nervous horse, trying to see if she were favoring any leg. Looked for swelling even as she focused on slowing her voice and her breathing. Halo continued to be agitated, but she was no longer nuzzling Honey, who was, to Tanner's total relief, beginning to move and moan a bit.

"Okay, baby girl. You and I are going to do a real slow dance, real slow so that Honey can get some help."

She didn't make a move. Just stood by Halo, looking at her and slowly weaved the loose bridle through her hand. She tried several times to lead Halo away, and Tanner was terrified to spook her in case she inadvertently trampled Honey.

"I'm in position," Tucker said, softly laying her hand on Halo's withers cutting her off from Honey.

She stroked and cooed and leaned against Halo's side, the pressure soothing but also forcing the horse to move step-by-slow-side-step, gaining precious inches of space so the EMTs could slowly make their way to Honey.

Tanner kept her focus on Halo, rubbing her neck, talking, and she was surprised to find Tucker staring at her. Tucker pushed up her Coach sunglasses, and Tanner saw Tucker's red, puffy eyes. It was the first time in a long time that Tucker looked human, looked like how Tanner felt deep down inside, a bit battered, vulnerable, but rising to the occasion, doing what needed to be done.

"You okay?" Tucker asked.

"Worried about Honey and Halo." *Obviously.*

"This remind you of your accident?"

"Not really. Probably would if I were normal." She mused, taking the olive branch Tucker offered. "But I've been to a lot of rodeos over the years. This isn't the first bad fall I've seen. Gonna be lots more."

Like maybe this afternoon with the bull finals, her stomach lurched sickly. No, Luke was fine. He was a champion. He wouldn't get distracted by anything. He wasn't as into her as she was to him. He was just a nice man so he felt bad for hurting her. He would be heading out in a couple of days anyway.

"You ever seen anyone you love fall and not get up?" Her twin demanded as they firmly, but slowly lead Halo to the exit gate.

"No."

She'd seen people she knew, liked, cared about, get hurt at rodeos, but loved? No. And she'd been at school in the midst of exams when her father had crashed and flipped over on his ATV while searching for a pregnant cow.

"I have."

Startled, Tanner tried to meet Tucker's vivid green gaze only she'd shoved her sunglasses back down and pressed more weight into Halo, freeing the EMTs to do their work without having to look over their shoulders constantly.

"How's Honey doing, Jake?" Tucker called out.

"Hey now, Tucker. Glad you're back," the young blonde barely out of community college said without looking. "You ever heard of HIPPA laws, girl."

"Heard about them and don't care. I helped train Honey with my sister here. Don't be letting me look bad now. She good?"

"I gotta keep my mouth shut."

"Wished you done that when I was babysitting you and I had to wash it out with soap more than once. Don't make me remind your partner that I changed your diaper and you got a mole on your—" She broke off as the partner, putting a neck brace on Honey, could barely stifle his snort of laughter.

"That's just mean, Tucker." A third EMT had backed the truck up between Halo and Honey and jumped out. "Good to see you home. Let me know if you need any of your moles checked out."

"Glad to see marriage hasn't spoiled your sense of humor, Dalton." Tucker sassed.

He grinned and joined his crew.

"Let's get her back to her stall," Tanner said.

"YOUR GIRL HAS balls of steel," Kane said to Luke as they watched the two women slowly back the horse, who didn't want to move, out of the arena. Their movements were coordinated, gentle, and clearly skilled.

"I don't see any balls." Parker said hopping up on the fence that separated the arena from the back staging area where the animals were brought in. "They got them in their pockets?"

"Some days," Kane said and Colt shot him a look, but Luke couldn't get into the mood.

He could barely take his eyes off of Tanner. He'd nearly spit out the damn five-dollar, almond milk latte Kane had insisted Luke suck down when he'd seen Tanner drop out of the stands and scramble over the fence and approach the clearly panicked horse. He thought he'd have a heart attack on the spot.

"Mom," Parker turned to Talon. "Did you hear about Honey and Halo? They went kaboom."

"That's why I'm here." She watched the progress of Halo and the two McTavish twins.

"Uncle Kane said they have balls of steel that they keep in their pockets some days."

"Uncle Kane?" Luke mouthed.

Nothing like taking things slow and easy.

"I want to do that, too."

"Sounds like a good aspiration," Talon said, biting her lip hard. "But, Parker, this is one of those colorful language things that you can't say at school or at a friend's house."

"Or in church," Kane added.

"Awesome!" Parker fist-bumped Colt and grinned at Kane. "Can I give Halo a treat to make her feel better?"

"Not now, buddy, and I'm going into super stealth work mode," Talon called out over her shoulder as she jogged to open the gate.

"I grew up on the back of a horse, herding cattle that didn't want to budge all the time, and watching Tanner walk toward that horse made me want to flip my shit," Colt admitted. "And today I had to watch Talon jam a syringe full of something into a bull's shoulder and that fucker was not standing still. Got no idea what you are all thinking, sitting on the back of one of those bastards. Crazy."

"It's a gift." Kane shot back, eyes on his brother, but his smile was long gone from his eyes.

Luke could feel his piercing gray beasts, so like their mother's, glue to his face, demanding answers. Was he ready to ride? Hell, yes. Nothing would stop him. Was he in top form? Honestly? No. He hadn't slept. He'd alternated between being pissed off at himself for not copping to knowing Tucker immediately and then with the Fates that had made each moment of this weekend a grudge match with those three bitches and then impotent fury with Tanner for being so unreasonable, and then anger with his anger because she'd been vulnerable, and he'd been a typical pig of a man picking a ripe fruit because it was easy.

And now?

He didn't know. He was going to ride and he was going to win and he was glad Tanner would be occupied with the horse she boarded and her injured friend so he wouldn't have to wonder where she was and if she were watching him because he now knew the answer was no.

"GO WATCH LUKE," Tucker said an hour later looking at her watch.

"No," Tanner said, watching Halo bang back and forth in her stall even though they'd lined everything with blankets. Each distressed knock notched up her anxiety.

Talon had found nothing medically wrong with Halo. Noah had run by and agreed. He and Talon had whispered together and then suggested they load up Halo and take her home, her stall and the comfort of familiar horses would ease her distress.

"I've got to get Halo home and who knows how long it will take to settle her."

"I'll take her."

"You're not familiar to her," Tanner said.

"I'm a freakin' horse goddess," Tucker said. "And Talon will come. She knows our stable. I texted Jorge and he called Alex at the ranch to line Halo's stall. Hell, I'll even sleep with her tonight since you and Talon snapped up the hottest men here and aren't willing to share."

Tanner shouldn't be staring at Tucker in outrage. Tanner knew Tucker spoke to poke people. But she had not snapped up anyone, dammit.

"And Kane Wilder is the biggest dud."

"Really?" Talon was packing up Halo's grooming kit and inserting her bridle in her mouth with Tanner as Tucker complained.

"Yeah. I've heard all these stories about his sexual prowess and I had a bit too much to drink last night, a bit. I wasn't drunk."

Tanner barely refrained from rolling her eyes. Barely since men were temporary and sisters were forever.

"And you know what he did?" Tucker demanded. "He took me back to his hotel room at the Graff. A suite! Ordered me a pizza and made me eat two slices and drink a bottle of water, not even sparkling, and then put me in bed and tucked me in like I was two and then left. He left. Who the hell does that? An altar boy or boy scout or total gay guy. Do you think he's gay?" Tucker perked up.

"I think he's a nice guy," Talon said. "I hope he comes back to Marietta to live when he's not competing. I think Colt's warming up to him a bit and Parker's in heaven. In just a week Colt's come back home to us for good, so Parker has a dad and a mom and now he has two uncles. Now all he needs are two aunts."

"Blech." Tucker made a throwing up motion. "Count me out, especially with Kane. I think something's definitely wrong with him. And I wonder what other aspects of his reputation have been exaggerated. Let's roll, Talon, so gloomy girl can go watch Luke get his ass tossed off Dervish."

"He drew Dervish?" Tanner felt like she'd just been tasered.

"Good luck. I saw his online stats and two videos while you were trying to get that hospital nurse to give you the goods on Honey. He's still a newbie but that dude can fly. Luke's in trouble. He's good but he's not Kane. That guy is a bull-whisperer. He's like one with the bull. He moves with the bull. Okay, shutting up now, because then I'll want to nail him again, and I'm not into being rejected twice. Go watch Luke. You can use the excuse that you are looking out for your bulls. See you at the ranch tonight if he's too banged up to be any fun." She winked.

Tanner felt a momentary tug of guilt. She'd known Honey since she'd been a baby. Tanner had helped Honey perfect a lot of her riding skills alongside Tucker. She'd raced with her in junior events. She boarded her horse, Halo. Responsibility pulled hard, but Luke pulled harder. She had to catch him before he mounted up. Wish him good luck or something in case it still meant something to him. It had not gone unnoticed that he had stopped texting.

So she gathered her frayed nerves and hurried over to the chute area. Damn. They were running ahead due to most of the cowboys being thrown off in the first second or two. Made sense. The bulls in the finals were higher ranked. She wished she hadn't been such a sniveling baby last night. She couldn't see Luke, but she could see Kane up on the pen saying something.

Totally not something that was sanctioned but Kane was an international bull-riding superstar. He'd won it all twice in the Vegas finals and he was just twenty-five. He could probably have gotten the rodeo crew to let him ride if he wanted.

Parker and Colt were leaning against the arena fence a little further away; Parker perched on Colt's shoulders. She wanted that. Tanner bit her lip. A man. A child. A sense of being part of something larger than herself. She'd felt the ranch and the animals and her successful breeding program would be enough but it wouldn't. She'd fleetingly touched the ultimate happiness and she was greedy. She wanted more.

She ran across the last few yards and clamored up the fence next to Kane. Her bull. She had a right to be here even though Josh was already up with the rodeo crew, but his job was watching out for the bull, not the cowboy. She caught Kane's eye but couldn't read his thoughts. Luke's head was down, his focus intense, wrapping his holding hand in tight. Left hand high in the air. Nod. Slide of metal. Tanner sucked in a breath and squeezed her eyes shut, her prayer for the man not the bull only she'd just thought the one word, please, when she heard a crash and a clang of metal that jarred her whole body and shouting and cursing and her eyes flew open in time to see the spooked Dervish whirl around and full body slam into the wall of the chute and then the gate before lurching off towards the rodeo clowns without Luke astride.

# Chapter Fifteen

SHE MIGHT HAVE screamed. She definitely jumped off, intending to do what… she didn't know… but before her brain formed a plan, Luke was up and scrambling up the side of the pen just as the cowboy got a rope over Dervish who turned quite tamely and went back in the gate like he was trotting off to dinner. That screwup would hurt his stats. Her eyes assessed Luke, who was bent over, Kane and Colt at his side.

She didn't belong. She knew she didn't, but she didn't care. She had to know he was alright.

"Are you hurt?" she demanded, practically body slamming him with her momentum and his arms came around her at the last minute and they bumped against the fence, which wasn't graceful but probably barely registered on the pain meter after Dervish's clumsy, disqualifying entrance.

"You want to go again?" The judge was asking, since anytime a bull touched the sides of the chute before being clear was a DQ, and the cowboy could get a do-over even though many of them were too banged up at that point to take up the offer.

"Are you hurt?" She demanded again, running her hands over his body looking for blood.

He was conscious, but not speaking, his features tight with pain.

"Want a medic?" One of the paramedics jogged up.

Again, Tanner felt the sharp jolt of missing Harry Monroe. She'd seen him at rodeos for years. He'd been a part of her life since kindergarten. And now he was dead.

Life was so precious, and Luke had just risked his. She could have lost him. Eyes squeezed shut she held him close.

"No medic." Luke shook his head.

He hadn't pushed her away.

"Luke?"

And then his eyes met hers and it was Tanner who couldn't breathe. She had been afraid that now every time she looked at him she'd think about him with Tucker. But it was just Luke and her there.

"I was so stupid to doubt you," she whispered. "To push you away, to let all my junk from my past intrude."

"What's it going to be?" the judge demanded. "You want to ride or you want to scratch?"

Kane looked at the score board. "You just have to stay on and you got it."

"What hurts?" Colt asked, Parker on the ground now, hopping excitedly back and forth from one foot to the other.

"Ribs, which you already fractured Thursday, thanks.

Added more to that count. Elbow. Shoulder. Wrist."

"I got tape!" Kane pulled a thick roll of medical tape out of his pocket and waved the medic over.

"You're a moron," Tanner told Kane. "He can barely stand. Luke, you do not have to ride again just because your so-called superstar brother's here."

Kane grinned and Luke laughed, spit some blood on the ground from his mouth.

"Hell, yes, I'm riding again," he told the judge. "And it's not because Kane's here. It's because I'm here."

And then he kissed her and Tanner totally melted into the kiss, forgetting Kane was steps away and Colt was watching. The whole rodeo crew was still perched on the fence waiting for the next bull and rider.

Parker was hopping around like a demented frog chanting, "Gross. Gross. Gross." And then. "Uncle Luke, that's so totally cool you're like spurting blood all over Tanner. It's like a video game mom won't let me watch."

She woke up out of her daze. "Luke," she whispered, touching the sticky wetness and then looking up at the cut over his brow where the butterfly bandage she'd placed Thursday afternoon hung loose and useless.

He laughed. "Guess I lost the bet and owe you dinner. Gonna have to take you up on your offer of stitches."

It took her a moment to remember their bet in her barn when she'd told him the bandage wouldn't last. She felt like a completely different person. A person who couldn't imagine another day without this man in it.

Tanner was barely able to peel herself off Luke long enough for him to take off his shirt. She winced at the bruises, but that was nothing compared to Colt pulling him up straight while Kane tightly wrapped his ribs with a cool efficiency that demonstrated just how often he'd done this, probably on himself and on others. Then he wrapped Luke's elbow and wrist. It was his hold hand, and Tanner's heart sank to her boots.

"I'm not sure about this," she whispered.

"Aren't you supposed to be rooting for the bull?" Josh and Jorge teased.

Tanner didn't take her eyes off Luke.

"There will be other rodeos," she whispered.

"But I'm here today."

She nodded. She got it. She'd grown up with and worked side by side with cowboys.

"With you." He slid a finger under her chin and tilted her face up to his and kissed her sweetly.

Tanner willed herself not to cry. He was tough and she had to follow suit.

"You want to do the honors or me?" Kane asked, holding up a needle and thread for stiches.

"Give it here," she said. "You'd probably do a bad job just to cut down on the competition for women."

"Think my brother's just taken his ass off the market, so more for me. And, Parker, you did not hear that."

"I did. I did hear it. You look like a pirate, Uncle Luke."

"Good. That was my second career choice."

Tanner felt like she was doing a good job channeling her tough, inner cowgirl as they finished bandaging Luke so he could stand up and flex his wrist without seeing stars and nearly toppling over. Yeah, she was good, until the bull draw came and it was the unfortunately accurately named bull she'd let Josh, in a moment of half drunken, all sleep-deprived madness, name Blitzkrieg.

"No," she whispered. "He's a one hundred percenter," she said, pressing her face against Luke's neck before having to let go because he was announced.

"Not anymore." Luke winked and mounted the fence.

Watched the bull angrily try to maneuver out of the pen before dropping down on him and getting his hand in position.

"Just eight seconds. Think of it as really fast sex like the kind you had as a teenager." Kane called down over the jostling and terse commands of the men pinning the bull into position.

"I'm not staying on for two hours," Luke shouted.

Kane laughed and dropped down next to Colt and Tanner.

Colt shook his head, his hands over Parker's ears.

"That's our brother, hard ass all the way."

Colt did a double take, and it finally sank in to Tanner that Luke had been dealing with some pretty heavy baggage himself this weekend learning about Colt so abruptly. One more tally in his long positive column where as she had come up short. Really, really short.

"Let's go watch." Parker grabbed her hand, and all four of them ran to the fence so they could see most of the arena through a gap.

Tanner bit her lip and counted the ticking seconds as the announcer re-announced Luke, reminded the crowd he was in first place and new to the Copper Mountain Rodeo and to give him a hand. And the crowd did. Up on their feet. Cheering. Whistles. She loved Marietta and all the people in it.

And Tanner felt a burst of pride so strong it nearly swamped her. And then she heard the familiar slide of metal and Blitzkreig, true to his name, shot out of the chute like a bullet and proceeded to thrash and twist and jump and ricochet all around the arena as if demonstrating to the crowd an example of a kick-ass ride, guaranteed to toss off any cowboy daring to try to stick it on his broad back. Only her cowboy, left arm high, body loose and fluid, stayed on and on. The buzzer couldn't be heard over the roar of the crowd, but finally the announcer calling out the Copper Mountain Seventy-Eighth Annual Rodeo had a new bull-riding champion, Luke Wilder, seemed to penetrate.

Luke hopped off and his eyes went from Blitzkrieg, who continued to run for a bit and charge at the clowns, to her. He mouthed something she couldn't hear, but his smile, and the heat in his eyes curled her toes and told her everything she needed to know.

Then he clamored up the fence like he hadn't been bashed up twenty minutes earlier and she met him at the top.

"That was crazy stupid." She breathed as their lips met.

"I got a date out of it."

"Yeah. Me, too." She continued to press kisses against his mouth and his jawline while her fingers wrapped hard around the railing so she'd remember he was injured and wouldn't grab him somewhere where it could hurt. "I'm falling in love with you, Luke Wilder," she whispered forehead resting against his, their breath mingling.

"Only falling?" he asked and then he dropped down on her side of the fence, taking her with him so they landed on their feet facing each other. "I definitely need to do better than that."

"Don't think it's going to pose much of a challenge for you," she said breathlessly, her words nearly smothered by the announcer and the crowd's cheers.

It was then she realized there was a line of people waiting to congratulate Luke, and he needed to go back into the arena for his interview, pictures, prize, and he wasn't going to be hers for a bit longer.

"You want to catch up later?" she asked. "Um, after." She waved her hand to indicate everything he still needed to do, and what she had to do. Her work today was far from coming to a close, even with a skilled and hard-working crew she trusted. And she knew winners of rodeo events didn't just say "thanks" and take off.

"Rather catch up now," he said, kissing her hard before turning away, jamming his hat down a little lower on his head. Then he turned back and the way he looked with his Stetson, sharp cheekbones, jutting jaw, and sensuous mouth flipped her heart. "Is it selfish for me to ask if you can wait for me?" His fingers trailed down her arm and tangled with her fingers.

"No." She held on to him tightly and could barely swallow around the lump of joy. "I'd love to."

THERE WAS SO much he wanted to say to Tanner, but most of it had to wait. He collected his prize, completed an interview with the local paper, and attended a short meet and greet with the county 4-H clubs, boy scouts and other locals. That had not been as socially strenuous as it usually was because Tanner had made the rounds with him, easily chatting, and casually slipping her arm around his waist.

It was the first time he'd felt part of a couple, and he could see why so many of his rodeo peers settled down after their first few wild years of playing the field. The idea of settling down with one woman began to take deeper root as Luke watched Tanner's soft, creamy cheeks, liberally dusted with freckles he never got tired of watching, glow with her enthusiasm. Her eyes sparkled and her slim, taut arms lent him strength. Even the idea of settling in Marietta no longer seemed distasteful. The few casual inquiries about any relation to Sam Wilder and Wild Wind Ranch were easily deflected, and he was starting to believe that even in Marietta he could be his own man.

All he'd ever wanted. To live life on his terms. And now that goal included Tanner McTavish.

As they made the rounds, it soon became harder to hide the extent of his injuries from both Tanner and his brothers. Brothers. He tested the word, and it no longer felt so foreign on his tongue. But now that the adrenalin and emotional rush of his win began to ebb, it became a challenge to stand straight. The ache in his ribs thrummed through his entire body making him ill, and the pain radiating from his wrist and elbow howled.

Tanner stole his hat, plopped it on her head, and then brushed his hair back from his forehead.

Then she smiled at head of the Chamber of Commerce, Jane Weiss. "Another wonderfully successful rodeo, Jane. Once again, you and the rodeo committee and chamber have really showcased our town and highlighted so many wonderful athletes, but Luke and I need to head out. I believe I heard something about dinner."

Smiling, she didn't wait for a reply but steered him out towards the parking lot. "I'll drive," she said. "You want to come?" she asked Kane and Colt.

"Only if we're taking this clumsy cowboy to the ER," Kane said, falling into step with her.

"You know it."

"I am not going to the ER," Luke said firmly, which would have carried more weight, perhaps, if he hadn't staggered and Kane helped to hold him up.

"I like it better when she helps." He grumbled. "But I'm not going to the ER."

"Don't make me toss your ass in my truck like our dog, Dude," Colt said. "Because I will and laugh about it later over a beer."

Luke lacked the energy to do any more than think about flipping him off, but there was Parker to consider. Shit. He was now an uncle. And a younger brother. And he had a girlfriend. And a shiny new buckle and his first Montana win.

"Best weekend ever," he murmured as Tanner helped him into the backseat of the truck so he could lie down if he wanted.

Tanner laughed "You think that's something, cowboy, just wait until I throw you an after party."

# Chapter Sixteen

"THIS IS NOT my first choice for a mea culpa," Tanner said softly, sliding her hand into Luke's. "It's an appropriate setting, but the hospital would have been better for you."

His fingers stroked her inner wrist the only indication that he was still awake. Tanner leaned up to look at him better.

He was so still and she swallowed. "Luke?"

"I'm awake," he said softly. "And the hospital would have sucked. This way we're alone."

Except for an agitated Halo, who was still nervously chuffing and shuffling about in the stall, but between going with Luke to the ER and waiting in agonized nervousness for the results of his X-rays and trying to check on Honey and coordinate by phone with Jorge and Josh, starting to load up the bulls without her, Tanner didn't feel like she could be away from the ranch, especially with Halo in such emotional circumstances. At least physically the horse was fine. Talon had reassured her over and over, and Noah Sullivan had swung by tonight as well.

Tanner had been unable to speak with Honey, but she'd been asked by one of the nurses to provide updates on the horse.

"Not exactly the Graff though." He mused, his eyes still closed.

"Ugh." She snuggled closer in the camp chair and adjusted the fleece blanket over him. "Don't remind me. I really blew that opportunity. It was like I was fourteen again. Instead of a scarlet letter 'A' I should have to wear an 'I' for insecure much for an entire month."

"Maybe a year," Luke said.

His lips twitched.

"Luke," she whispered, her finger lightly tracing his collarbone, visible in the V of his shirt.

She needed to touch him but was so afraid of hurting him. She'd seen him without his shirt in the ER, and he was covered, just covered, in bruises. How he'd managed to roll away from Dervish's hooves and hop the fence and then fifteen minutes later hold on for a full eight on Blitzkrieg she didn't know.

"I promise to never, ever do that again."

"What part, cowgirl? There are some parts of this weekend I definitely want to repeat on an infinite loop."

She gently smoothed his hair back from his forehead, tracing his widow's peak over and over with a shaking finger, thrilled that other than the cracked ribs and hairline fracture in his wrist he was fine.

"My allele doing okay?"

"Luke. Don't joke." She didn't know if she should laugh or cry. "I'm trying to apologize for being such an idiot. I promise I will never again shut you out like that without letting you explain, especially when you are competing. I was overreacting and insecure and it was completely unfair to you."

*Dangerous.*

Kane had been right to be so angry with her. She still couldn't think about their exchange without flushing with shame. He'd been looking out for his brother and she'd been looking out for her pride, nursing a hurt born so many years ago.

His eyes opened and again she was caught in his heated honey stare. She could look at him all night. All the rest of her life.

"You weren't an idiot," he said. "I should have told you. I didn't realize your sister was Tucker T until Kane told me after he interrupted us in the trailer. By that time I'd already realized you had a bit of a rivalry or bad blood or whatever with her. Our attraction was so new, and I had never felt like that before. You really did a number on me, Tanner McTavish. I could barely remember my name. I had planned to keep it casual until I told you but then at my trailer you opened the bathroom door naked and…"

"I was not shy that night." She cuddled closer to him in

the camp chair, but was careful, not wanting to jar his ribs or his injured arm. "I was actually trying to be bold like my sister. Take what I wanted and, Luke, I wanted you. I want you."

It took all her self-restraint to not bury her face in his chest. To hold on and never let go.

"I could have lost you." Her voice broke and the tears flowed freely.

"Not a chance." His voice was deep and his arms around her strong. "I have you. I'm not going to blow it now."

Tanner leaned over him, unable to resist. She kissed him, a whisper of a kiss, afraid of hurting him, but his uninjured arm snaked around her, splaying on her back to pull her in closer and deepen the kiss. Tanner moaned.

"Oh, my God! Get a room!" Tucker came around the corner, lugging a thermos, sleeping bag, lantern, and tote. "You two are making me ill."

Tanner sprang away from Luke and Tucker laughed.

"Not like I don't know what's up." She rolled her eyes and plopped down everything next to Halo's stall.

"Did you finally get an update on Honey."

"I got more than that." Tucker smirked. "I snuck into her room and I think that doc Sean Gallagher was doing more than a medical examination if you know what I mean."

"Tucker, not everything is about sex." Tanner was horrified.

The look Tucker shot her and Luke could have curdled

rubber.

"Says you. Honey's going to be fine. She'll need time, but she'll ride again." Tucker closed her eyes and sucked in a breath.

"What aren't you telling me?" Tanner asked.

"I tell you everything," Tucker said coolly, pulling on a fleece vest.

The emphasis was on "I" and Tanner didn't miss it. Damn, Tucker was prickly, and Tanner just felt too raw and emotional to deal with it.

"Get the hell out of here. I have a date with a horse."

"But Halo is my responsibility."

"Sitting in a barn in a camp chair when the temp's going to dip down low isn't good for broken bones or for true confessions so stop being a martyr, and you stop thinking you're Supergirl. You got a bedroom here."

"Yuck. Dad's across the hall and old fashioned."

"Never stopped me."

Tanner knew. She'd had to sleep on the couch more than once because of Tucker's late night adventures since they shared a room until Tanner had left for college. Luke was looking uncomfortable, but whether it was all injury related or partially Tucker related, she didn't know, but the adrenalin must be long gone, and he wasn't due for pain meds for another hour.

"I can fix you something to eat," she told him.

"Got it." Tucker handed them a tote. "Picnic. Go to

Luke's trailer. That at least has a…ahhh…" Tucker seemed to gather her thoughts, and Tanner realized she'd been braced, holding her breath. "Before you start in on me about responsibility, Talon is coming over tomorrow to check on Halo and Noah Sullivan is coming over before noon so we are done here. Tucker T out." She made an explosion sound and mimed dropping a microphone.

Tanner didn't need to be told twice. She was not proud of the fact, but she really didn't want to sit in a small space with Luke and her sister. It wasn't that she didn't trust his feelings were real, but they were new and hopefully growing and she didn't need to expose him to Tucker in such a potent dose again.

She needed to get over that. She kicked herself. Definitely get over it, but not tonight. She took the tote and planned to help Luke to his feet, but he was already up, his features tight and hard to read. His arm was in a sling and his ribs had a medical brace wrapped around them. She tried not to hover, knowing cowboys were tough and when they were around their women even tougher.

They didn't talk on the drive to the fairgrounds. She thought he might fall asleep. Instead he watched her drive and the warmth and intensity of his scrutiny had her breath feathering in her throat and her body going pliant and liquid with desire.

Totally inappropriate for the situation. The man could barely stand. He needed a bed and time and to be left alone.

She lectured her libido, which ignored her. His hand touched the side of her face and, without thinking, she turned and kissed his finger.

*Down girl. Eyes on the road.*

Hard to do when Luke's hand spread out on her thigh. God, that felt good. The strength. The size. The warmth. The power. The skills he had. A sound escaped her, one of longing she couldn't have held back in. It was exhilarating, this desire, and terrifying. Like a drum in her blood. Want. Want.

"I want to make love to you," he said.

The words had the power of whiskey, straight to her head. Someone had to be a realist or she'd crash the truck.

"That might be a little ambitious, Luke."

So why were her panties already wet. Poor man. If he didn't shut up, she'd jump him the minute she cut the engine.

"I need to." The words were stark.

Hung there.

Where the hell was the air? She pressed the power on the window letting the cool night air swirl in, trying to dissipate the desire, except the wind only made her curls blow wildly around her head. She'd forgotten that while he'd been sitting up in the ER getting checked out he'd finger combed out her braid with a whispered "please." The way he adored her hair still felt strange, but she loved the way he looked at her, didn't quite trust it all the way, but she was trying to get there.

"Will you let me in?"

As if she could ever deny him anything. The power he had over her was heart-stopping. Stunning. And not something she could grab the reins back from even if she wanted to. She'd always been an all-in person. Barrel racing. Healing. Remaking her life as an academic. Rebuilding the ranch and setting lofty goals. Loving Luke.

"Always," she whispered. "But I don't want you hurt."

"I'm tough," he said, a little arrogantly but with a smile and for a moment she had a glimpse of a playful Luke, a little like his younger brother. "We may have to be a little creative though. You might have to do some of the work."

She stopped the truck, played with the keys, wondered if she should just go for it or try to talk about the future, but Luke was already climbing out, fishing for his keys. She popped out fast, grabbing the tote of food and supplies Tucker had given her along with her overnight bag. Luke jammed the keys in the lock, just as the door swung open.

Kane, wrapped in a towel, making what appeared to be a smoothie.

"Hey, girl," he said, making no move to cover up even slightly.

Was that a tattoo of a… she turned away, face flaming. She was not going to ogle Luke's younger brother. Let lightning strike her right now! Imagine if Tucker had come instead of Tanner. Tucker would have climbed him like a jungle gym.

"Bro."

Luke cursed.

"That's no way to be." Kane handed Luke the smoothie. "I figured you'd be back for some privacy," he said smugly. "Drink that. It's full of antioxidants. It's my go-to drink when I'm hurt. I'll give you the recipe and, before you continue to curse me out, mom's here too, waiting for you."

"Luca!"

Samara Wilder rushed out of the trailer and gently touched Luke's brow near the stitches and then she kissed first one cheek and then another. Her hands, slim and graceful, wrists covered with silver bangles, skimmed Luke's bandaged wrist, and the arm in the sling. Tanner stared at the woman she'd heard so much about. In her mind, Samara Wilder was the wild teen girl, running off with a rodeo star when she was fifteen. She was for Tanner frozen in time. The brief handshake a few days ago in the trailer hadn't done her justice.

"Mom, it's not a big deal. I'm fine."

Tanner nearly bit back a laugh. So here was the drama queen, fireball mom who'd kicked Luke's ass in a bar fight and sided with a man she didn't know, but who ended up to be her long lost son. Yup, in true telenovela style, she was beautiful. Elegant. And she didn't look at all like she could have three grown men as sons.

Samara slid a look at Tanner and she notched up her

chin. She was not going to apologize for interrupting the family reunion even though Samara was clearly waiting to talk to Luke. Probably alone.

Luke slipped his arm around Tanner's waist.

"This is Tanner McTavish," he said. "You met her a couple of days ago."

"Not senile, Luca," Samara smiled, and she went from beautiful to stunning, and her smile was so much like Kane's. "Bruce's daughter, yes. You run the ranch he still thinks he runs. Men."

"I knew I'd like you," Tanner said, smiling.

"Oh, no double-teamed, brother," Kane said. "I'd better get dressed."

"Why?" Samara demanded. "You like showing off your body. You did even as a boy."

"Mom," Kane and Luke said at the same time.

"Definitely getting dressed." Kane slammed the trailer door leaving the three of them out under the stars. Most of the trailer rigs had already pulled up stakes and driven away.

"Did you talk to Colt? Will he see me yet?" Samara's voice was low, broken.

Tanner's heart spasmed at the pain in her voice. Here was a woman who had lived life on her own terms. Who was beautiful, smart, and successful but even she had not been spared deep sorrow and loss.

"I think, Mom, you need to give him time," Luke said tiredly, leaning his weight more fully against Tanner.

"That girl he loves, with all the hair, will she help? Should I approach her?"

"Talon," Tanner said. "Yes. She wants to meet you. She wants Colt to meet you, too. He's getting there. He's—" How to describe him.

She barely knew him, but Talon's glowing words as well as the other ones about how he had trouble sleeping, trouble shutting down, rang in her head.

"He's been through a lot. He was in the army for twelve years. Lots of deployments and has only been home a week. He needs time. He's a very private person. I knew of him in high school, but even though he was on the football team and a top player, he stayed to himself." She hesitated to add the last part. "He didn't have an easy time growing up with Sam Meizner who wasn't quite right. He drank and had problems with… well, with a lot of things. Probably depression. So Colt had a lot to deal with."

She didn't want to hurt Samara or expose Colt, but she needed to know where he was coming from.

"But I am his mother."

"You're not, Mom. You're not his mom like you are Kane's and mine, so you don't have some right to barge in. You can't make it happen. You're going to have to let him come to you if he wants."

"But he's my son. He needs to know me. He needs to know what happened."

"You can't push like you push everything," Luke said

tiredly.

Samara Wilder's blue grey eyes sparked with indignation, and she tossed her mane of long, silky, black hair. "I am not leaving town. I don't care what my father's done out of spite, denying his grandchildren their mother, father, identity and birthright. I am home. And I will meet my son."

Tanner admired her determination, but she was feeling that Luke should get horizontal quickly. She could feel the strength in his body ebbing. Only Kane was in the trailer. And Luke's mother had just determined that she was going to stay. Did that mean here, in the trailer?

"So..." A fully clothed Kane opened the door. "No dairy or beef for a few weeks," he said. "Too inflammatory. I've already emailed you my injury recovery nutrition menu. It's full of antioxidants."

"So is my fist. Get out of my trailer."

Kane laughed. "Offer's still open." Kane dangled the key to his room at the Graff in front of them. "Since ya'll look like you made up. I even packed an overnight bag for you like Mom would have done if I'd let her near your stuff."

"You'd better have packed condoms," Samara said, arms folded across her chest.

Tanner swallowed hard. Luke glared. Kane grinned.

"Although, Kane, sweetie, maybe you should leave those out. I'd like some grandchildren before I'm senile."

Tanner choked this time. Senile. The woman looked thirty but had to be at least forty-five.

"Plenty of time for that." Tanner, face flaming, grabbed the bag and the key from Kane. "Lovely to meet you."

Sort of.

She linked her fingers with Luke's and headed for her truck.

"Tanner, can we walk?" he asked.

"You must be hurting."

He touched his chest. "More here."

"What?" She hurried forward, reaching out for him. "I can take you back to the ER. Another X-ray. Or an MRI. Maybe they missed something."

"What I'm feeling won't show up on a scan," he said, taking her hand and pressing it over his heart. "I want to walk with you in the night with the moon, maybe some stars and a lot of quiet."

She shouldered his bag, and grabbed her overnight case and then slipped her arm around his waist. Walking at night with this man sounded perfect.

"Not just tonight," he said softly, "but for longer."

Her eyes searched his as they reached the bridge spanning the Marietta River that led to downtown. Was he asking if she were up for the walk and stars tonight or for many nights in the future? She practically crossed her fingers and wished like she had when she'd been five. *Oh, please, oh, please, want me. Love me.*

"Luke." Her heart felt too full to speak.

He reached into his pocket and pulled out two pennies.

"Make a wish?"

Tanner took the coin. It was as if her every dream, her every wish had just been granted, as if her ordinary life just became magical. She couldn't really comprehend it. She turned around, but instead of closing her eyes, she watched Luke. Made her wish for a forever with him and watched as he smiled then made his own wish.

With his working hand, he turned her towards him. His beautiful, golden gaze searched her face while his hand reverently touched her cheek, lips, hair. He stood close. She could almost feel the heat of his body.

"I'm just so overwhelmed by my feelings for you," she finally said, wanting to say more but not having the words.

He cupped the back of her head and then let his hand smooth down her spine. "Yeah, intense. Sideswiped me, too, but I've got you."

LATER, AFTER A shower where Tanner had soaped and kissed her way over his body like she owned it, which she did, and making him forget a lot of his bruises, Luke reclined, naked on the bed and watched her prepare a snack from the food Tucker had packed them.

"It would taste better if you were naked," he said.

She laughed. "It's going to taste fine." She adjusted the tie on her robe from the Graff so it gaped a little.

She felt bold and reveled how she could see his eyes heat

instantly with desire. She had a strong body, athletic and slim but nothing any guy had ever seemed particularly fascinated by or with.

"And you'd better eat because you need your strength because I'm not done with you."

"Bring it on."

But there was a knock on the door.

"If that's Kane, I will kill him slowly." Luke started to get up, totally naked and totally delicious despite the wrapped arm from elbow to wrist and ribs, but Tanner rolled her eyes and marched over to the door, pulling her robe tight, and answered it.

Room service. Champagne. A fruit basket and cracker and cheese plate. And then dessert. A chocolate something and then blackberry cheesecake.

"Okay, Kane has at least one redeeming quality." She snagged the card and read his message. "Can you open this." She handed the server the champagne. "I've never opened one of those suckers."

Done. And gone. Alone.

She poured two glasses and handed one to Luke.

"Should we toast your first place win?"

"I'd rather toast us." His eyes were a little wary as they walked over her face, down her body and then back again.

"Luke, I know it's fast," she said, "and you'll travel a lot. You don't have to commit to anything. And my dad, well, he"—she bit her lip and tears filled her eyes—"he said something about thinking about selling the ranch. I can't believe that. I can't believe he'd even think like that. The Triple T is one of the earliest ranches in the valley, not a founding Marietta ranch, but from the late 1890s. He's just so obsessed with not having sons. It makes me so mad. It makes me—"

Luke turned her face up to his, and kissed her cheeks, tasted her tears, pulled her close, and she wrapped herself in his warmth, feeling safe and secure even though the bottom might truly be dropping out of her life.

"So there might not be that much to commit to," she said in a small voice.

"I want to commit to you," he said, "not a ranch. Not a town. You."

"It's so soon." She looked up at him, hopeful, but still feeling anguished. "I know you've been with—"

He laid his finger over her mouth. "That's the past. We are the future," he said. "We can build our future together if that's what you want."

Her eyes searched his. "I do." She sounded reverent.

"You are everything to me, Tanner. You're so real. Between my mom, who was so shattered by her early experiences with her dad, and my dad and Kane and his damn career I've had so much drama. One-ups-manship. Attempted manipulation. You are so honest. So natural. I know I gave you reason to doubt me. I'm so new to the concept of a relationship that lasts, Tanner, but I want to be good at it. I want to be what you need. I want to be what you want because I want you, Tanner. Now and always. You're my cowgirl"

She leaned forward and kissed him, not the passionate, drugging kisses that had made her head swim and her knees go weak in the shower, but more like a promise. Reverence.

"I want you too, cowboy." She didn't break eye contact. "From the moment I first saw you at a rodeo after a ride, and now that I know you and have been in your heart, I want to stay here and love you and be loved by you forever."

She laid down carefully next to him.

"I love you Tanner, but, no," he said.

"No what?" Her heart kicked up anxiously.

"Robe off."

She smiled. And started to shrug it off.

"No."

She stopped, thrilled by the firmness of his voice.

"Stand up. I want to watch."

Heat pooled low in her body. Who would have thought she'd respond to that edge of dominance in his voice and expression, but Tucker felt like liquid. She slid off the bed, faced him, and dropped the robe. She swallowed hard. He'd seen her naked before, but he'd been standing up touching her, not watching like she was on a stage.

"Now my belt."

She felt like all the air in the room was gone. "Luke?" she asked shakily.

He reached for the velvet box that held his winning buckle from the rodeo.

"Oh. My. God." She mouthed the words.

She'd been joking. He was totally serious. Tanner felt thrilled to her bones. And terrified. She hadn't had many partners. And the sex had been straight forward. But she was a cowgirl. She was Montana born.

She swished his belt out of his jeans and walked over, hand out for the buckle. The light in his eyes and the appreciation stamped on his beautiful face settled her nerves. She was wet and excited and her hands were shaking, but she slid the leather in, thinking about him sliding in something else hopefully soon. She looped the belt around her waist.

"Now your boots."

Her breath feathered and she felt another pulse of liquid between her thighs. She watched him watch her as she slid her bare feet into her boots.

He was so hard and so beautiful, and the sight of Luke Wilder aroused was the most spectacular thing she'd ever seen.

"Hair."

She slid out the elastic on the end of her braid and then finger combed her hair into its wild riot of curls that sprang around her head, she thought like Medusa, but Luke was so aroused her could barely sit still on the bed so she let go of one last hang up. For him she could do anything. He made her feel powerful even when he was ordering her around, and she couldn't wait to take over.

"I'm going to have you," she said boldly. "Tonight. And every night I can get you." She walked toward him, each step deliberate.

"I'm all yours," he said wrapping his hand around his erection.

"Don't," she said, eyes on her prize. "Mine."

His eyes looked like they'd been lit with a match, and his smile was just as heated. "Come get it." He taunted, removing his hand so she could see how badly he wanted her.

She thought of all the silly lines she could say, but instead just settled on honesty. She loved Luke Wilder. All of him. And she wanted to show him in so many ways.

"You're glistening." He licked his lips. "I want to taste you. Please, Tanner, come here."

She came. She kissed him, tasted him, made him beg, played with herself, letting her fingers rub her clitoris and dip into her slick channel while she straddled him, and let him lick her fingers after she orgasmed, and then she rolled a condom over his exquisite length and straddled him.

"I hate that I can't touch you like I want," he whispered, since one arm was immobilized, so only one hand could grip her hips.

"We're doing just fine," she said, tracing his mouth with her finger. "We'll be creative until you heal."

"I need to be inside you. Please. Please, Tanner."

Eyes holding his, Tanner slowly lowered herself onto

him, gasping at the sensations rolling over her body, his size, his everything. He filled more than her body. Her heart and soul and mind felt full, connected to him in a way she'd never felt before.

"Luke," she said, amazed, gripping his hips with her strong inner thighs as she felt him deep in her core.

She leaned forward to catch his moan in her mouth and began to move, slowly at first, letting the heat build between him, and then faster, amazed at his strength as with one hand he guided her to a rhythm that sent her careening over the edge with a few thrusts, just with the angle he held her hips, and then he continued to slam himself up into her over and over again in a primitive rhythm that had her body and soul and mind rejoicing.

God he was strong, and that turned her on, but it was so much more. He was so much more.

"I love you," she whispered as he continued to thrust her up towards her peak yet again, and she had no idea how he could coordinate himself since she was shaking and seeing stars and biting her lip to keep from screaming out. But he was so much more than this. His beauty. His sexuality. His physicality and strength. "You're everything." She moaned as she could feel herself about to fall apart again and all she could do was cling like a monkey with her arms and her legs. "Everything."

And then she felt herself explode around him again, and this time she dragged him with her, feeling him spasm deep within her where he belonged. She continued to hold on, pressing kisses on his shoulders, neck, her fingers tracing circles on his chest. “Everything,” she said again.

He held her as they slowly settled, stroking her hair, and kissing her, drugging kisses over and over again.

“Cowgirl, I’m barely getting started.”

## The End

Other sizzling romances by Sinclair Jayne…

**The Christmas Challenge**

**Seducing the Bachelor**
*The Bachelor Auction Returns series*

**Wrecked**
*The Sons of San Clemente series*

**Broken**
*The Sons of San Clemente series*

If you enjoyed *Want Me, Cowboy*, you'll love…

## The 78th Copper Mountain Rodeo Series

Book 1: Catch Me, Cowboy by Jeannie Watt

Book 2: Protect Me, Cowboy by Shelli Stevens

Book 3: Want Me, Cowboy by Sinclair Jayne

Book 4: Love Me, Cowgirl by Eve Gaddy

*Available now at your favorite online retailer!*

# About the Author

Sinclair Jayne has loved reading romance novels since she discovered Barbara Cartland historical romances when she was in sixth grade. By seventh grade, she was haunting the library shelves looking to fall in love over and over again with the heroes born from the imaginations of her favorite authors. After teaching writing classes and workshops to adults and teens for many years in Seattle and Portland, she returned to her first love of reading romances and became an editor for Tule Publishing last year.

Sinclair lives in Oregon's wine country where she and her family own a small vineyard of Pinot Noir and where she dreams of being able to write at a desk like Jane Austen instead of in parking lots waiting for her kids to finish one of their 12,000 extracurricular activities. …

Find her on Twitter@SinclairJayne1

Thank you for reading

## Want Me, Cowboy

If you enjoyed this book, you can find more from all our great authors at TulePublishing.com, or from your favorite online retailer.

84709697R00175

Made in the USA
San Bernardino, CA
11 August 2018